C000128707

A Chapter on Love

Visit us at www.boldstrokesbooks.com

A Chapter
on Love

by

Laney Webber

2019

A CHAPTER ON LOVE

© 2019 By Laney Webber. All Rights Reserved.

ISBN 13: 978-1-63555-366-6

This Trade Paperback Original Is Published By
Bold Strokes Books, Inc.
P.O. Box 249
Valley Falls, NY 12185

First Edition: February 2019

THIS IS A WORK OF FICTION. NAMES, CHARACTERS, PLACES, AND INCIDENTS ARE THE PRODUCT OF THE AUTHOR'S IMAGINATION OR ARE USED FICTITIOUSLY. ANY RESEMBLANCE TO ACTUAL PERSONS, LIVING OR DEAD, BUSINESS ESTABLISHMENTS, EVENTS, OR LOCALES IS ENTIRELY COINCIDENTAL.

THIS BOOK, OR PARTS THEREOF, MAY NOT BE REPRODUCED IN ANY FORM WITHOUT PERMISSION.

CREDITS
EDITOR: RUTH STERNGLANTZ
PRODUCTION DESIGN: SUSAN RAMUNDO
COVER DESIGN BY MELODY POND

Acknowledgments

To Radclyffe and the welcoming community at Bold Strokes Books, thank you. I'm so happy my novel found a home with you. I'm not usually a lucky person, but I hit it big with my editor, Ruth Sternglantz. Thank you, Ruth, for the care and feeding of my dream. Thank you to Melody Pond for designing a cover that makes me smile each time I look at it.

Thanks to Patrick Hummel at New Hampshire State Parks and John at Wolf's Neck Woods State Park in Maine, for their generosity and patience with all of my questions. My beta readers, Franci McMahon, Elaine Burnes, and Ana B. Good, gave me the good, the bad, and the ugly in wonderfully constructive and instructive ways. You have my deepest gratitude.

To some very special women in my life. The women of the real-life Purple Tent Book Group, thank you for continuing to meet after all these years and thank you always for your generous support. I carry the laughter and memories with me. The GCLS Writing Academy workshop leaders, writers, and queerleaders— Hey, Ona! Hey, Tammy! Hey, Cindy! Hey, Joy! Hey, Theresa! To Lee Lynch and Ann McMann for not going easy on me. To Heidi and "Hey, it's Laney Webber!" Kimmie, Cindy, and Trish. Thank you for being my best friends and my biggest fans.

Thanks to my family, who never stopped waiting for that first book to be published. Here it is, Mom! Thank you, Jillian and Nathan. Whether you know it or not, you have been my guiding lights and the reason I did almost every scary and good thing in my life. Thanks to Kyle for keeping me in the groove, being the best example of persistence, and for our yurt yaks. Treyton, for tech talks, helping my brain switch tracks, and understanding what an anti-ice cream social is. Flynn, for being equally at home in joy and questions.

A special thank you to the women of the former Artistic Amazon bookstore in Portsmouth, NH, where I discovered the world of lesbian fiction and a community.

Finally, to the person who changed my life forever, and makes the stars seem possible to reach, the love of my life, my Louie. Thank you for always believing and for being game to do all the wacky things I asked of you during the creation of this book. You are most definitely the whole package.

Dedication

To my Wonder Woman.

Chapter One

Jannika Peterson had blind date remorse. Last week she'd been in a hopeful mood when she agreed to go out on her fourth blind date in two months. But after four straight days of cold rain, her last drop of hopeful ran down the catch basin.

She looked out the window of The Pageturner and rubbed the short hairs on the back of her neck. The bookstore closed at one on Sundays, and all she wanted was to go home, have a cup of tea, and read book reviews. She put her laptop and copy of *Booklist* in her tote bag.

The bells on the bookstore door jingled. Jannika turned around. A tall young man with blond dreadlocks stood in the doorway.

His words came out in a rush. "Are you closed yet? I need a book. It's like...an emergency."

Jannika smiled and waved him in. She loved book emergencies.

"I'm so glad you're not closed. I need a book that's, like, different, you know? I looked on the stupid interwebs, but I can't find anything. I want something that's going to help, you know? Something that will help me help the planet." He scrunched up his face.

"Are you looking for something about the environment?"

"No, more like about our connection to the environment." He looked over Jannika's shoulder toward the bookshelves.

"Come. Follow me." Jannika was happiest when she was connecting books and people. She'd learned to read when she was four, and for her the next best thing to reading was sharing her love for a book with another person. She'd always loved recommending books to her friends in school and discovered her talent for matching books and people during her first year of college when she took a part-time job in a tiny bookstore in Portland, Maine.

She ran one finger across the spines of the books as she walked. She stopped and pulled a book off the shelf.

"Here you go—*Ishmael* by Daniel Quinn. It's older, but I think you'll like it." She smoothed her hand over the book's front cover.

"Huh, isn't that, like, from *Moby Dick*? I didn't like that book."

"It's not about *Moby Dick*—it's a book about questions." Jannika pointed to the back cover of the book. "The author deconstructs the myth that we are separate from nature and does it in a unique way. I think you'll like it. Is there anything else I can help you with?"

"No, this looks great. Thanks for staying open for me. How much is it?"

He followed her to the front of the store and paid for the book. She locked the door behind him and turned over the *Closed* sign. It looked like the rain had finally stopped. She still had enough time to go home and get ready for her date with Brenda. She hoped it wouldn't last long and paused at that thought. That wasn't a good sign. Her string of bad blind dates had become a running joke between her and her best friend, Marcy. The humor covered up her fear that maybe there was no love of her life out there.

A montage of date bombs played in her head. The woman who thought she was from another planet and they were destined to be together; the movie date who held on to Jannika's coat for the duration of the movie because she wanted to feel close to her; and the frightening blind date that extended into four days when the woman locked herself in a local motel room and serial called and texted Jannika.

She grabbed her bag from behind the desk and her leather jacket from the coat rack and headed out the door and downtown.

❖

Lee drove her forest green Toyota truck down Avery Lane, the shortcut road that ran from Grangeton to Route 101. Her fingers tapped the top of the pizza box in time to WOKQ's best country hits of the seventies. She sang along, making up words when she didn't know the lyrics. Her friends took good-natured jabs at her for her taste in music, but she loved the she-done-him-wrong songs and would sometimes make up her own in the shower and while driving. It wasn't les-correct, but she didn't give a damn.

Lee stepped on the brake. Avery Lane was a great shortcut, unless you hit the red light. She turned down the radio and saw two women on the corner outside a coffee shop. They were either having a lovers' quarrel or were on a really bad date. Whatever the opposite of sexual tension, that's what was rippling through the air from the couple—they were obviously together but just as obviously apart. The light turned green and Lee turned the music up again and hit the gas.

She'd moved to Fairfield, New Hampshire, a couple of months ago from Maine. The only people she knew were her friend from college, Hannah, and her old work buddy Steve, a retired park ranger. Hannah was coming over tonight. Lee was in charge of pizza, and Hannah the movie. Fairfield's town center provided just the basics—a post office, the large white clapboard town hall that housed both the library and the police station, the Fairfield Congregational church, and DJ's Store. The nearest pizza place was in Grangeton.

Lee drove down the maple lined driveway to the little farmhouse she rented. Hannah's headlights flickered in her rearview mirror. She parked, grabbed the pizza box, and waited for Hannah, who parked behind her truck.

"Hannah girl!" Lee reached one arm out to embrace her friend.

"I can't even tell you how good it is to see you." Hannah hugged Lee, then stepped back. "Look at this place. I always wondered what was down this long driveway. This is sweet. I bet I know what's in there." She pointed to the red and white barn to the right of the small white farmhouse.

"You bet. It's one of the reasons I took this place, so I could have room for all of my woodworking stuff. Let's eat, then I'll show you everything."

❖

Jannika drove through Grangeton and into Fairfield, turning right onto Myrtle Street. The beams of her headlights bounced off the sliding glass doors of her cottage. She rested her head on the steering wheel.

Dating was exhausting. Each time she went out with a woman, she hoped for a good match, and each time she was disappointed. She was tired of downloading her life résumé across a table from someone she knew wasn't a good match— just like she knew when a book wasn't a good match because she felt it in her gut. She didn't think she was too picky. She was just being careful since her breakup with Joanne. She wiped her wet cheeks with the back of her hand.

All she wanted was to be in her house surrounded by her things. The driveway gravel crunched under her boots. She went inside and sent a text to her best friend Marcy.

Another date—another disaster.

A few minutes later her phone chimed with a text from Marcy.

OO.

That was their code for *otherwise occupied*. She knew *OO* meant Marcy was with one woman or another and not in town. Marcy didn't go out around town for fear her parents or their friends might find out she wasn't dating men since her divorce from Greg.

Jannika put her kettle on for tea, then changed into some yoga pants, a T-shirt, and a big old blue and red flannel shirt she'd found at the Methodist Church thrift store. She rolled the sleeves of the flannel shirt halfway up her forearms. She liked to pretend it was her father's shirt. The image she had of her father was a cross between Harrison Ford and Steve Martin. Jannika didn't know what her father looked like. She didn't know his name. The subject was and had always been off limits in her family.

She pulled the flannel shirt tight around herself like a hug and let the heaviness of the fabric comfort her.

The red kettle whistled. She poured her tea and stuck a frozen vegetable lasagna into the microwave. She ate her dinner at her grandmother's plain birch kitchen table. Her grandmother refused to be called Nana or Grandma but insisted everyone use the Swedish, Mormor. Jannika loved to cup her hand around a rounded corner of the table and imagine Mormor setting places for her mother and Aunt Gunnie when they were little girls on the farm in New Sweden, Maine.

Thinking about Mormor and the potato farm helped fill the hollowed-out place inside of her. Her grandparents and the rest of her family weren't big talkers. Their economy of living was matched by their economy of words. Her family didn't talk about feelings. The way they showed love was to do things. Aunts and grandmothers baked and made casseroles. Uncles and cousins and grandfathers fixed things, or helped you load hay, or cut wood.

She gave the table a pat and flipped open her notebook. October was a busy month at the bookstore. Several book groups were meeting, the Simon's Warehouse sale was next weekend, and the window displays still needed to be changed out for fall. The action of making lists calmed Jannika better than any pill.

She added *Call back Darlene* to her list and waggled her pen back and forth in her hand. Darlene was a customer who had come into the store about a year ago and left a voicemail message late yesterday afternoon when Jannika was busy with customers.

When she'd first seen Darlene, a succession of book images shuffled through Jannika's mind like a deck of cards. Darlene talked a lot and fast. Her hands hung still at her sides. Everything about her was still except her voice. At first, Jannika couldn't pin down any book titles that would fit what Darlene thought she was looking for. It took Jannika a few questions and a few minutes of chatting about other things to recommend Paul Coelho's book, *The Alchemist.*

Jannika loved reading reviews, sorting through used books for treasures she knew her customers would love, and buying books, but her favorite part of her job was reader's advisory. It was an intimate few minutes between strangers. People came in the store when they were looking for comfort or trying to figure out a problem or learn something about themselves. Many people came in to try to find copies of books they had read when they were younger, and some wanted a great mystery or suspense story. As they described their quests and Jannika asked questions, bits of information came together in her mind like pieces of a jigsaw puzzle. As soon as she could see enough of the picture, she knew which book to recommend.

She smiled and took a sip of tea. Her dating life might be dismal, but she was happy every hour she spent at The Pageturner. She underlined *Call back Darlene* twice and closed her notebook. She had an early morning meeting tomorrow at the bookstore with Betty Busby, the leader of one of the monthly book groups. Betty Busby was the last person she wanted to see tomorrow.

CHAPTER TWO

Jannika ruffled her hair, then grabbed her travel mug, a tote bag full of book reviews, and her laptop. She juggled her things from one hand to the other and unlocked the side door to the old brick building.

She whispered *Thank you* each morning when she opened and *Good night, little bookstore* each night. This secret daily ritual began after her Aunt Gunnie told her the owner of The Pageturner was looking for a new manager, and Joe Bosworth hired her a year and a half ago.

Joe had greeted her on the day of her interview with a clipboard in one hand and a timer in the other. He asked her to sit at the big desk at the front of the store and fill out a run-of-the-mill employment application. He took it when she was finished, passed her the clipboard and a pen, and said, "There's a list of titles of books on one side and authors of books on the other. You have to fill in the blanks. Give me the authors to the books, then flip it over and see how many titles you can come up with next to each author's name. I'm timing you. Go."

It was one of the strangest interviews she ever had. Her boss was a big man. Not fat, but tall and large-boned. He had started the bookstore for his daughter, but she'd moved to Portland, Oregon, after two years of the book business. Joe ran the business for about a year but felt trapped in the store. One of his buddies told him he should hire a manager, and there Jannika was, wildly writing down the names of authors and book titles, so she could get her dream job. And it was. The minute she walked into The Pageturner she felt like a long-lost key and the bookstore was the lock. She fit.

Jannika set her bag and tea on the big oak desk at the front of the store. She turned on lights, adjusted a display, and tapped wayward books back onto their shelves. A flash of purple caught her eye. She turned to see Betty Busby, dressed in a lilac polyester pantsuit with matching lilac socks in white vinyl sandals. A purple and green flowered scarf was tied around her neck in a neat knot. Betty's silver hair was a teased and lacquered helmet. Clip-on pansy earrings completed her ensemble. She tapped at the door with what looked to be the arched back of a cartoon black cat on a stick.

"Just a sec. Good morning, Betty, how are you?" Jannika opened the door and took one of the three bags Betty carried.

"I've talked with the girls and we've got a great plan for this year. We've decided on a Halloween theme. We'll dress up the corner of the store with these decorations, and we want to read something spooky, but not violent. You know we don't like violence, Jannika, or cursing or"—she lowered her voice to a whisper—"anything sexual."

Betty pulled orange and black cardboard decorations, plastic ghosts, and a jack-o'-lantern with battery operated candles out of a large bag.

Jannika eyed the props and inwardly sighed. "It looks like you had a great time at Michael's. Since we only have a couple of weeks until Halloween, I thought a short story might work for everyone. How about 'The Legend of Sleepy Hollow'?"

She chose her words carefully. Betty Busby was a townie. She'd grown up in Grangeton and the farthest she had traveled was the hour trip to Concord, New Hampshire. She helped organize fundraisers, sat on the select board at one time, and now wrote a column for the local weekly paper, *The Bugler*. Jannika liked Betty but learned she needed to set some limits and set them with care. She didn't want to end up the subject of this week's newspaper column. She'd witnessed that with Trisha Pusie from the flower shop down the street.

Last summer, a not-so-blind blind item about a certain flower shop in town was mentioned in Betty's column. The owner was described as a know-it-all who liked to boss her customers around rather than give them good service. Tricia's experience reminded Jannika to try to stay on Betty's good side, or she would have to spend her time fixing the damage Betty did with her column instead of selling books.

"We used to read that in school. I haven't read it for ages. A short story. Hmm, I'm not sure, but we'll try it. So, what do you think of my decorating ideas? I think the other gals will love it." Betty clapped her hands.

"Betty, my only concern is the other book groups. What if they want different themes?"

"Like what? It's October, it's fall, it's Halloween. Who could have a problem with that? Who do you think might have a problem with that, Jannika?" Betty placed a hand on her polyestered hip.

"I don't think anyone will have a problem Betty, and I love your theme, but I am thinking about the Purple Tent Book Group. One of the members doesn't celebrate holidays, and I know how sensitive you are, and you wouldn't want to—"

"Me? I'm not sensitive. I think all you young people are too sensitive. They're Halloween decorations, Jannika, and our ladies will love it. It'll bring back memories, make them feel young. Maybe we'll dress up. Oh, wait until I tell Mildred! We're going to dress up and make our own trick-or-treat goodies for the night." Betty turned to leave. "It's all set. It's all planned. Thanks for your help. We'll see you the last Friday of the month as usual." She put down her bags of decorations. "I'll leave these here and be over a few days before to decorate. Oh, it's going to be a hoot.

I'll tell the girls to pick up the story here. Oh, and Jannika, don't think I didn't see that article about you in the *Concord Monitor* last week. But we'll talk about that later." Betty waved a hand over her lilac shoulder on her way out.

Jannika's stomach did a flip as she grabbed the door on its return and opened for business. Managing Betty Busby was always more labor intensive than she anticipated. She was happy Betty didn't want to decorate today. There were four people waiting for Jannika to open, and one of them was an artsy looking young woman with short, messy-in-that-cool-way blond hair, carrying a good-sized box of books.

Jannika had a love/hate relationship with boxes of used books. Along with moldy and dirty books, she had found a cat turd, a handmade icon of a saint, a half bottle of perfume, melted candles, and a filthy baby shoe among other non-book items. She could usually tell at first glance if she needed the box of vinyl gloves behind her desk. After a few months at The Pageturner, she began to take photos of her book box goodies. She wasn't sure what she was going to do with the photos, but collecting them took her mind off the ick factor.

"Put these here on the desk and let's have a look."

"My grandmother passed away and I didn't want to throw these out. You can have them. I don't want store credit or anything. She used to read to me each time when I visited." The woman stroked the spines of the books with long fingers fitted with multiple silver rings.

In Jannika's mind an intimacy existed between most people and their books. She stepped with care into the space of the relationship of book and person. She thought it was like trying to put your hand through a bubble and not have it burst, but have the bubble absorb you into itself, making you part of the relationship. She could tell who wasn't quite ready, and would try to persuade them to take at least some of the books and wait a while if possible. She also could tell who was ready or needed to part with their books. But she couldn't grab the box from them. To her that would be ripping a loved one from the arms of another.

"Are there any special books? One or two you might like to keep?" Jannika asked.

"No. I don't know. Maybe?" The woman shrugged and touched the books again. "Maybe this one," she said, pulling out a book with a slightly worn cover, its dust jacket long gone.

"Ahh." Jannika smiled. *"The Wind in the Willows."*

The young woman looked up at Jannika. She had very blue eyes.

"Yes. Thank you so much for encouraging me to look them over again. I'll keep this one. I'm Amy, by the way." She extended her hand.

"You're very welcome." She shook Amy's hand. "I'm Jannika."

Jannika put the box of books on the floor behind her desk.

"Hey, Nick." Marcy, Jannika's best friend, came into the store with a paper coffee cup in each hand. "Oh, sorry, didn't mean to interrupt." Marcy put both cups on the desk and cracked open the plastic lids.

Amy looked over at Marcy. Jannika watched Marcy dive right into Amy's ocean blue eyes.

Marcy extended her hand. "Uh…I'm Marcy. I stop by whenever I'm around to fortify Jannika with some caffeine. In the form of tea of course. I like to think I'm doing my bit to support local bookstores by keeping Jannika functioning. Looking at books all day would make my head spin."

Jannika watched her normally smooth-talking friend stumble over her words.

"I'm Amy. Nice to meet you."

Marcy kept holding Amy's hand.

"Those are some interesting rings."

"I have a friend who makes jewelry and she loves to try out designs on me."

Marcy and Amy relinquished their hands in slow motion. This was better than watching a rom-com.

"Could I find your friend's work around here?" Marcy took a step closer to Amy.

"She has a studio in the White Mountains in a little village. You've probably never heard of it. Tassy Brook, over by Littleton?"

"I know Tassy Brook. My family has a camp about fifteen minutes from there."

Jannika watched this exchange with keen interest. Marcy usually kept a careful distance from anyone local, for fear her mother or father might catch wind of the fact their daughter was a lesbian.

Jannika saw a customer near the home improvement books who seemed to be looking at the front of the store, seeking assistance.

"I'll be right back," Jannika said.

Marcy and Amy didn't so much as glance her way. Jannika thought she could have jumped up on the desk and danced, and they wouldn't turn their heads. The customer waited at the end of an aisle with a book in each hand.

"Hi there. How can I help you?" asked Jannika.

"Which one of these is better?" the older man asked. "Nona, my wife, wants a book on greenhouses. Do you know anything about greenhouses?"

"Why don't we bring them over here to the table and take a look," Jannika said. She led the way to a table by a window and moved a chair out of the way. "Does your wife like to garden?"

"She used to be out in the garden, but ever since she retired, all she thinks about spring, summer, fall, and winter is what she's gonna buy from the nursery and where she's gonna put it in the yard. Now she wants to grow her own and wants to draw up some kinda greenhouse for me to build her this winter." He hitched his pants an inch or two up his big belly.

"This one. I think she'll like this one," Jannika said. She pointed to *How to Design and Build Your Garden Greenhouse.* "Is there anything else I can help you find?"

"How much is it?"

Jannika looked inside the cover where she or the manager before her had penciled in a price in the upper right corner. "Twelve dollars."

"I noticed you could use yourself some shelves in the back there. I'd be happy to make you some. Maybe for some book credits for Nona. She's the book person in the family. Name's Tommy." He put out his hand for Jannika. "I did some work for your boss on his house a few years back, and I've got some nice wood. Take me, I don't know, a day or less to get some shelving in there."

They did indeed need the shelves. "Sure thing, Tommy." Jannika handed Tommy the book.

"I can come the end of the week."

"Sounds like a plan."

Jannika liked to barter for services she or the store used. Her boss encouraged her to do this, as long as the bartering didn't go over a hundred in sales. He considered it her monthly bonus and thought it was good community relations. She traded mystery novels for fresh eggs, and Clive Cussler books for syrup. Jannika had never met Tommy's wife. Tommy came by often to pick up books Jannika picked out for her, but he never said why she didn't come to the store herself. She must be able to get around if she gardened, Jannika thought. Maybe she was claustrophobic or allergic to dust.

She often made up stories about her customers' lives. Aunt Gunnie would take her to the library when she was a little girl. When they got home, they would have rosenmunnar cookies and make up stories about the people they had seen. Aunt Gunnie would tell Jannika she was her little *rosenmunnar*, her little red mouth, and would playfully scold her for licking the jam out of the middle of each Swedish thumbprint cookie before she ate it.

Jannika wanted to give Amy one last chance to accept an offer for her grandmother's books.

"Well, Amy," Jannika said, putting her hands on the box of books, "are you sure you don't want a store credit or cash for these?"

"I don't want anything. I just didn't want to throw them away." Amy's voice trailed off. She glanced over her shoulder at Marcy, who—Jannika knew—only pretended to look through the free books bin over by the door.

"Thanks. These are great books. Here you go." Jannika handed Amy her grandmother's copy of *The Wind in the Willows*. "Don't forget your book."

"Oh, right, thanks. It was nice meeting you. I know my grandmother's books are in good hands." Amy again glanced back, no doubt searching for Marcy. "Thanks again." Amy walked toward the door.

A blur in the shape of Marcy flew past Jannika's desk and caught up with Amy before she left the store. Jannika watched her friend as she stacked books on her desk.

"Hey you," Marcy said. She touched Amy ever so lightly on the elbow. "See you next week? You have my number?"

"I can't wait."

"I can't wait either."

Amy left the store and Marcy rushed over to Jannika.

"What did I just do, jeez." Marcy slapped the palm of her hand against her forehead.

"What *did* you just do?" Jannika pretended to brush something off her shoulders. "Brushing off wayward sparks." She smiled. "Sarah comes in at ten today. She'll be here any minute. Let's go get brunch at the Over Easy. You owe me some in-person condolences after my disaster last night with Blind Date Brenda."

CHAPTER THREE

The little brass bells on the bookstore door tinkled, and tinkled again. The door opened halfway, then shut, then opened again. Jannika watched long blond hair fly into, then out of the doorway. She rushed over to help with the door. Her one and only employee had her hands full of tote bags filled with... something.

"Oh gosh, goodness," Sarah struggled to catch her breath. "The universe wasn't cooperating today. I think Mercury is in retrograde. First my car wouldn't start—my neighbor had to come over and jump it—then the gas pump was out of order, then I couldn't find a parking space. I even invoked my parking angel. Nothing. And I bought these for the store."

Sarah dropped the bags. She reached into one and pulled out a small, perfectly round pumpkin and flipped her hair over her shoulder.

"Aren't they nice? Very womanly. I thought you'd like them, Jannika."

Jannika smiled and caught Marcy's eye. Sarah was forever finding womanly or femme-centric things to bring to the store.

"Thanks, that was very thoughtful." She helped Sarah pull pumpkins out of the bags. "Can I leave you with the store for an hour or so? Marcy and I thought we'd grab some brunch."

"Oh, for sure. But don't touch anything mechanical. It's not the day for mechanical things, trust me." Sarah frowned and shook her head at them.

"Not to worry Serenity…sorry, darn, Sarah, I mean," said Marcy.

"That's okay, Marcy, but I'm trying to distance myself from my old name. You remember my parents. They mean well and everything, but growing up with that name was no party. Every time someone calls me by the name my parents gave me, it makes it harder for the universe to take my old name back. My old name gets held here in space and time—you know what I mean?"

Sarah outlined an invisible box with her hands.

"Okay, Sarah. I promise I'll try to remember," Marcy said.

"I know you were my babysitter and everything, so I get you might hang on to my name longer, but I'd like to let it go."

"Totally get it, Sarah," Marcy said.

"Be back in about an hour." Jannika slung her jacket over her shoulder.

As soon as they stepped onto the sidewalk, Marcy slapped her thighs and stomped one foot. "Damn, Jannika. What am I going to do about Amy? Isn't she gorgeous? Isn't she wonderful? Did you see her eyes? Oh no, that's a bad sign. Isn't it?"

"Whoa, my friend. Everything will be all right. Walk with me. Let's go get some sustenance."

They walked on the uneven brick sidewalks past Bronislaw's Bakery, Stone Bridge Jewelers, McCray's Rare Books, and Tricia's flower shop—Pusie's Posies, before turning down a cobblestone alleyway to the riverfront restaurant. They'd missed the breakfast rush and were seated in a booth overlooking the river, but they weren't here for the view this time.

"Okay, Jannika. The date sounded bad, even for you, the queen of bad dates. Let's talk about that first, then the Amy thing."

"She wore a Porky Pig jacket and thought I was staring at her boobs when I noticed Porky. She made some snarky comment and called me babe every other sentence."

"I know how much you love to be called babe, babe." Marcy chuckled. "Sorry, did you leave after the third or fourth one?"

"No, then we walked down to the antiques place, you know, the Quonset Hut place, and it was almost closing time. She made a big show of not wanting to leave and told me if we got locked in she could break us out because she'd done it before. I think she was trying to impress me, but no, just no. It was awful."

"Whoa, that's kind of creepy," Marcy said.

"Kind of?"

"Definitely creepy and definitely bossy. I know how you feel about bossy women. Two words. Origami class," Marcy said.

Jannika laughed and tossed a piece of her straw wrapper at Marcy.

"You're the one who got us in trouble," she teased Marcy.

"I don't even remember what was so funny, do you? We kept laughing, and it sure as hell pissed off Miss...What did you call her?"

"Miss Stay on Task. *Ladies, you are not staying on task,*" Jannika said with a nasal tone. "You snorted."

Their laughter was interrupted by a pale, very skinny, very young waitress. Her staff T-shirt with the words *Over Easy* and a picture of a giant fried egg hung off her in folds. She took their order of two breakfast sandwiches, coffee for Marcy, and tea for Jannika.

"I knew we'd be best friends that day," Marcy said.

"Me too," Jannika said. "Thanks for trying to cheer me up. I know everyone wants me to get out there, but I hate it. As of last night, I've taken a no-more-blind-dates vow. And the cherry on last night's sundae was the truck with Maine plates that drove right past me at the end of the date. I freaked out a little. Which is really dumb. There are hundreds of cars around with Maine plates. It was a bad date and the truck reminded me that I'm still alone over a year after the breakup."

"Crap, Nick, I'm sorry you had another bad one. Maybe not a vow, maybe a little break? I know that shit wears you out. I think you have some kind of beacon that attracts, shall I say... unusual women?"

"Thanks, Marce. All I know is, I'm done for now. How about you tell me about what just happened at the store with the very fetching Amy while I eat my sandwich, I'm starving."

"Did you see her eyes?"

"Yes, I saw her eyes, and I also noticed the way they looked at you. I felt the wave of heat across the room. What about your *I never date local women* rule."

"Exactly. Why did I even talk to her? I know I can't go out with her. I've been this route before, dating a local. I'm not going to sneak around and pretend. I'm not going to ask her to do that either. I need to call her and say I got caught up in the moment. I forgotten I have a girlfriend or wife or something."

Marcy's hands played with the straw in her glass of water, stretching the little ribbed bendable neck in and out like an accordion.

"See this? This is my heart. I meet someone I like, who I think I want to get to know, and zip"—she squished the ribs of the straw back together—"my heart closes down because of the reality of my family. Who doesn't know Barclay's Burgers? They're all over New England."

"Marce." She reached across the table for Marcy's hand. "How long will you keep doing this? I know you want to go out with Amy." Jannika lowered her voice. "You're my best friend. I love you. It hurts to see you always shutting down, turning away from love, from life. What can I do to help? I'll do anything to support you."

"Jeez, Nick. Maybe it's time for me to leave Grangeton and start a life somewhere else." Marcy looked over Jannika's shoulder at the river.

"So you're going to run away? From your family, your job, your friends, Amy—from your life? I know everyone knows your family, you're Marcy Barclay of the Barclay's Burgers chain. I can't imagine how public your life feels anyway."

Marcy put her head in her hands.

"What do you really want? Marce, what is your heart saying?"

Marcy raised her head and looked at her with wet eyes.

"I want to live like you do. I want to feel like a whole person, not a person split in two. The good daughter my parents see, the good straight girl who just hasn't found the right man after her divorce, and the horny lesbian who trolls the bars in Provincetown and Ogunquit to let go. I want to be me. I want to go after this Amy with the crazy beautiful eyes and the voice that…Did you hear her voice? Did you see how beautiful she is? And…oh…" Marcy shook her head and sighed.

"Your parents."

"My parents," Marcy replied. "I can't. I've lived like this for so long. I don't know where to start. I'm afraid of what they will do, of how they'll hurt me."

"What about one at a time? What if you told your mom? You told me you used to be close." She leaned toward Marcy. "How much do you want to see Amy again?"

"Dirty pool, Nick. That's dirty pool."

"You know I'd never push you into anything. And I know we've had this conversation before. But I want to see you happy, and I've never seen the look on your face you had when you talked with Amy. I couldn't take my eyes off the two of you."

"Maybe I could talk to Mom or at least start talking about something with her. We've grown so far apart. The part of me that isn't terrified wants her to know who I am."

"I'll be there for you. Whatever you need. Whatever you want," Jannika said. She looked over Marcy's shoulder and smiled as Amy walked into the café.

"Thanks." Marcy said. "What are you smiling about? Where's our server?" She looked past Jannika, waved, and nodded for the check.

"Amy's here and she's walking this way," Jannika said.

Amy smiled at Jannika.

"Hi," Amy said.

"Hi again," Marcy said. She stood and wiped her hands on her napkin.

"I picked up a smoothie up front and saw you back here and…" Amy shifted her weight and took a step back. "Sorry I interrupted. I wanted to say hi again. Which is kind of silly because I met you about an hour ago."

"No, no, we were about to leave, and I'm glad you came over," Marcy said.

"You are?" Amy said.

Jannika watched Marcy's gaze travel over Amy.

"Very glad," Marcy said.

"I'm looking forward to your phone call," Amy said. She reached over and touched the cuff of Marcy's jacket sleeve with one finger. Two kids ran past the booth, and Marcy and Amy both turned to face the booth, bumped shoulders, and laughed.

"I think we might be blocking traffic," Marcy said.

"I have to run now anyway—I just wanted to say hello," Amy said.

"Who's taking this check?" The skinny waitress waved their check in the air.

"I'll get it." Jannika held out her hand.

Jannika walked behind Marcy and Amy to the front of the café. She paid the check at the counter while Marcy and Amy talked behind her.

"See ya," Marcy said.

"Can't wait," Amy replied. The door swung shut behind her.

Marcy opened the door and held it for Jannika. Her eyes were still fixed on the retreating figure of Amy.

"I have no idea what's happening, but she's too amazing to say no to, rule about local women or no rule. I'll walk you back to the store, then I'm off to meet Dad," Marcy said.

As they passed Pusie's Posies, Jannika pointed at bunches of flowers in the window. "I want to go into Pusie's and pick out flowers for my date. I want to actually *like* my date. There was that one woman that I dated a few times. I liked her, but she went back to her ex. But I didn't feel heartbroken. I was disappointed, I wanted to see where it went, but...you remember."

"I remember. I always thought you were trying to force that one. She sounded nice, but not your type. More my type, a party girl."

"I don't know how you go out on all those dates."

"They're not dates, that's how, kiddo." Marcy elbowed Jannika. "I've got to be careful, but you don't. You can go out with anyone, anywhere."

"But I want it all, the whole package. I want the fireworks, someone who gets me, and someone who I'll want to spend the rest of my life getting to know." Jannika looked down at the brick sidewalk as they walked up the hill. She pushed her hands in her jacket pockets. "Silly, huh?"

"And I thought my pool of fish was small."

"I'm serious." Jannika stopped and looked at Marcy.

"I know, sorry for joking. Tough subject matter for me. But I guess you can't give up, right? If that's what you want, then you can't just stop dating, because how will you ever find your Ms. Whole Package?"

"Maybe just a small break from dating, like you said."

"That's the stuff. I'll keep you posted about Marcy-world. Sorry about the disaster date last night, truly."

"And my meeting with Betty B this morning." Jannika exaggerated a frown.

"Ouch, been a rough twenty-four for you, my friend."

"But the Purple Tent meets tonight, so somehow it all balances out." Jannika sighed and smiled.

Chapter Four

Lee picked up some fresh eggs and local bacon from a farm stand on the way home from an early morning meeting at Watt's Lake State Park. She wanted to help the staff close up the park for the season. The campground was closed, but the park remained accessible to hikers, and then snowshoers and cross-country skiers during the winter. Her staff would leave next week and she wanted to get to know them now, before they reopened in the spring.

She had the remaining ingredients for a frittata at home. Whenever she cooked, it reminded her of cooking in the big farm kitchen with her mom. Doing something physical always calmed her, and today she felt a bit jangled about going to the book group. Well, not the group itself, that was fine. She was looking for a way to meet people in the area and her friend Hannah had invited her to come along. But then Hannah had casually mentioned that Jannika, the bookstore manager, ran the group.

That was what jangled her.

How many women could have the name *Jannika*? Could it be the Jannika she knew eighteen years ago when she was a Girl Scout camp counselor at Camp Pine Knoll? She'd be what? Thirty-five? The thought of a grown-up version of Jannika made Lee's palms sweat. She couldn't remember the last time that happened.

Just thinking about camp took her down memory lane. She'd taken the camp counselor job right out of college—winters, she'd worked at Sunday River ski resort, and summers at several Girl Scout camps in western Maine. Then a friend of her mother's told her about an opening for a state park ranger at Durkee State Park in the Casco Bay area. That job had been love at first sight—for seventeen terrific years. Time flew. She sighed and rubbed her knee. Her new position as the park manager at Watts Lake State Park was an opportunity to work more closely with people who loved the outdoors. Plus, she was in charge of a staff again. Lee liked to be the one making the decisions and setting the tone at her park.

She drove down the long dirt driveway to the farmhouse. The maples were almost at peak color. There were a few leaf peepers out on the road here and there, but by next weekend she would have to use the back roads. She'd rather be on the road a bit longer, than be behind some flatlanders taking pictures and weaving all over the road.

She brought the groceries in and unloaded the wooden signs that her permanent staff helped put in the back of her truck this morning. Some routing work and paint would freshen them up. The physical labor would take her mind off the *What if it is Jannika?* question that circled her brain again and again like a kid's toy racetrack car.

Customers piled into the bookstore Monday afternoon like it was a tourist stop. Jannika helped them find what they were looking for and tried to figure out which book they wanted when they described it.

"That blue book. The one with the blue cover and some mountains on it, I think. It might be new. I don't know." The woman fluttered her hand around her face like she was fending off mosquitoes.

"Did you see it online? Or on TV?"

"I think it was on one of those morning shows. The author is that woman who does that talk show about health? It's on in the afternoons."

"Is that the woman who talks about food and nutrition and the brain?"

"Yes." The customer perked up. "And how you can improve cognitive function with what you eat."

Jannika smiled while she groaned inside. "We don't get a lot of new books in the store, but I could try to find the title for you, and you could order it at Little River Books in Dover, or online. We might have something else for you, though."

"You mean, you don't have new books?"

"Once in a while a customer will bring us a new book, but usually we don't—we're a used book store. But I can show you a few other books like hers if you'd like."

"Sure. I'm already here."

"Come with me." Jannika brought the woman down the center aisle and pointed to a group of books on the top shelf of one of the bookcases. "Here they are. I'll get these down for you and you can take a look at them." Jannika passed two of the books to the woman.

"Oh God. These are perfect! I didn't know there were other books like this. Are there more?"

"Only one more." Jannika handed the woman the book and saw Sarah coming up the aisle.

"Vicki is here. She wants to see if you need anything for tonight," Sarah said.

"Can you please tell her everything is all set for the Purple Tent book group. I've got next month's books set aside, but I'm busy right now. Tell her I'll see her tonight. Thanks." Jannika turned back to her customer.

"I want all of these. Where do I pay you?"

"Right at the big desk," Jannika said motioning to the front of the store. "I'll be right there." On her way up, she was stopped briefly by a couple who wanted dog training books. When Jannika got to her desk, Sarah was busy ringing up a short line of people who clutched their finds. Jannika loved watching people treasure-hunt in the store.

Jannika knew used book stores were closing all over the country. People liked the convenience of choosing books online. But she thought nothing compared to spending an hour or two in a bookstore, new or used, and browsing until that special book called out to you to pick it up and take it home. She was glad there were still people who felt the same way she did.

As Sarah waited on the last customer, Jannika glanced down the four aisles of the store and went to the back to break down the table displays and make sure there were no stragglers or nappers. She checked the little children's book alcove on the left and the reading corner on her right with its comfy chairs.

"I'm grabbing the orphans," Jannika called. She picked up stray books that customers had left around the store.

"I've got the door," Sarah replied.

"Thanks, I don't know what I'd do without you. You are always so patient with everyone who comes in the store." Jannika put her armful of books on the desk.

"I love my job, and I love my boss. You have the best energy of any boss I've ever had," Sarah said. She swung her backpack on. "'Night, Jannika."

"Good night Sarah, see you tomorrow." She wasn't sure how many bosses Sarah could have had in her twenty-six years but smiled at the sentiment.

Jannika turned over the *Closed* sign and locked the door again. She popped her leftover black bean and sweet potato burrito into the microwave and grabbed several folding chairs from the closet near her desk area. She used her leg to push the display tables near the reading corner to the side and set up the metal chairs. She pushed the three ever-popular stuffed chairs from the reading corner to complete the circle for the book group. Then she ate her supper and finished preparing for tonight.

She rarely sat still anymore, even for a meal, even though she knew she would get a stomachache from all that moving and eating. Sitting still meant thinking, and thinking these days meant thinking about her ex, Joanne.

But she was looking forward to tonight. This was her group, the Purple Tent book group. She'd reached out to a local lesbian support group when she first came to town and invited them to start a book group. Members came from all over the Seacoast area. Nina and Lauren drove north from Newburyport, Massachusetts, when they weren't traveling. Everyone else was from New Hampshire. They brought food to share, talked about whether deodorant caused breast cancer, who in the group actually ate kale, and what wine went with trifle. They also talked a little about that month's book. Like most book clubs, there was always a bit of tension between those who wanted to spend more time talking about the book and those who wanted to socialize. Their laughter was a prescription for Jannika's heart.

Jannika cast a glance at the clock on the wall behind her desk and saw someone already at the door. She grabbed her keys and let in Paula and Priscilla—or the two peas, as they were known. These two warm, generous women were like two peas in a pod.

"Nick, you look fantastic as always," said Paula.

"Look at her hair—wouldn't you love to have your fingers in that hair?" said Priscilla.

"Pris, the only fingering of hair by you will be done to me," Paula said, tossing her nonexistent long locks.

Jannika and Priscilla laughed and Paula leaned in to Priscilla for a kiss. These two women gave Jannika something to hope for. When she watched them, together for eighteen years and married for six, she saw everything she wanted in a relationship.

The door behind Jannika opened, and the rest of the book group came through the door in a cacophony of sound, carrying tinfoil wrapped pans and bowls.

"Brownies!"

"Soup—where is the plug for this Crock-Pot, Nick?"

"I've got sandwiches."

"And I brought a friend who is new tonight," Hannah said. "Everyone, this is Lee. She just moved here. And she's even read the book. Even though it was a big one. What was *The Paying Guests*, about a thousand pages?"

"Five hundred and seventy-six. But I would do even more for Sarah Waters," Paula shouted from across the store.

"You'd do Sarah Waters," Pris yelled back.

Jannika smiled. And Lee chuckled.

As a chorus of *Hi Lee*s came from the women at the front of the store and the back, something about the woman tickled the files in Jannika's brain. Lee looked like she could be on the cover of *Outdoor Woman*. The hiking boots, jeans, and muscled thighs made Jannika take a longer look than she usually gave most strangers. Above the jeans, under a navy quilted vest, she wore a long-sleeve cotton jersey under a button-down maroon shirt with the sleeves rolled halfway up her lightly tanned forearms. Her face had seen some weather, and Jannika felt her breath catch. This woman was gorgeous.

Several women hung their jackets on the coat rack at the front of the store, exchanging dishes with each other as they did. They laughed and played pass the pans. It didn't make any sense, but it had happened on the first book group night and was now a ritual.

Jannika couldn't shake the feeling she knew Lee, and her mind kept shuffling her memory deck of possibilities. Where could they have met? But more than that, her body had the visceral feeling she got when she was near an ex-lover, the little physical buzz of one body knowing another body. Why was that happening? She knew she would remember if she had made love to this woman—she was striking. Her arms and legs were lean and strong, and she had shoulder-length golden-brown hair. Lee looked like someone who either climbed rocks or lifted them for a living. Jannika's heart beat faster and the buzz of recognition wouldn't stop.

"Jannika?"

Hannah was waiting expectantly for her to answer a question. A question she hadn't heard.

"Oh gosh, sorry. What were you asking?"

"Never mind. Let's get our chairs."

"Should we discuss the book first, then eat? Or eat and discuss the book?" Jannika asked.

"We tried that before," Pris noted. "If we eat first, we never talk about the book."

"I'm pretty hungry," Hannah said.

"Then I guess we'll eat first. First let's have Lee introduce herself, and we should do the same." Priscilla sighed.

The rest of the women found chairs and sat down in the small circle. They looked at Lee.

"Hi, everyone. Thanks for letting me tag along with Hannah. My name is Leslie Thompson, but my friends call me Lee. I've known Hannah since we were in college in Maine. When I told her I had the opportunity to be stationed in New Hampshire, she said, *Come on down.* I was a park ranger in Maine and moved down about two months ago to manage a park near here, Watts Lake State Park."

Vicki and Linda nodded their heads in recognition.

"Nick, I mean Jannika's from Maine," Linda said. "We all call her Nick, well, everyone but Hannah. She likes to use everyone's full given name."

Laughter rippled around the circle.

Jannika's ears rang and a stampede of wild horses filled her heart. It couldn't be that Leslie. The Leslie she had the huge crush on at camp. Leslie the Girl Scout camp counselor. That was eighteen years ago. The summer after she turned seventeen. The room seemed to tilt a little then right itself. Jannika looked over at Lee.

Lee beamed a smile across the room and gave what Jannika thought was a nod of recognition. Jannika heard the sounds of the book group discussion but the words floated around and past her like dandelion puffs. She tried to look like she was listening to the conversation, but her mind went back to that summer, comparing that Leslie to this Lee who sat across the circle from her. This woman who had her legs stretched out in Jannika's bookstore. This woman who just laughed at something the Two Peas said.

"I'm ready for some grub," Hannah said.

"Count me in." Linda launched herself out of her chair and toward the food table.

Vicki followed her girlfriend, who was piling her plate high. "I love a woman with a good appetite," Vicki said. "If you know what I mean." She kissed Linda on her cheek. "Hey, Nick, did you make those cupcakes again? Those cupcakes make your mouth water and your pussy too." Vicki looked at the line of women behind her and let out a wolf whistle.

"Oh, I can't take her anywhere," Linda said. She took Vicki's elbow and steered her back to the circle of chairs.

Lee made her way around the other women and stood behind Jannika in the food line.

"I knew it was you, the minute I walked in the door of this store," Lee said.

"You remembered me?" Jannika looked straight into Lee's honey-brown eyes. She rubbed the back of her neck and shifted her weight from one foot to the other.

"Yes, I remember you. Who forgets Girl Scout camp? And how could I forget someone with the name Jannika? You're definitely all grown up, aren't you?" Lee's eyes traveled down to Jannika's feet and back up to her face.

Jannika could feel the heat rising in her neck and face. She turned to speak to Paula who was next to her in line, but Paula and everyone else were back at their chairs with their food. She and Lee took turns with the spoons and spatulas, filling their plates. Jannika fumbled with the utensils, and at one point Lee took the spoon from her and put potato salad onto Jannika's plate. She heard a muffled *shh* as she and Lee came back to the group with their plates and sat down to eat.

"Jannika is a book psychic or a book doctor or somethin', the way she matches people with books," Vicki said. She balanced her plate of food on one crossed thigh.

"And she's *single*," sang Hannah. "Lee's single too, just saying."

"And Hannah is our resident matchmaker, in case anyone missed that." Paula pointed her fork at Hannah.

Hannah knew their lesbian family tree. Who broke up with whom, whose ex was now with someone else's ex, who was looking, and who might be looking.

"I'd like to hear more about how you match people with books sometime," Lee said. She shifted in her chair and faced Jannika.

Jannika noticed the Two Peas looking at her and at Lee and back again, then whispering something to each other. Those Peas never missed a trick. She tried to focus on her food and the discussion around her. This grew more and more difficult now that her brain and her body knew who Lee was. Her body was on hyperalert. Each time Lee moved in her chair or looked her way, butterflies took flight in Jannika's stomach. This was silly, she told herself. She was seventeen. Lee shifted in her seat again and her forearm brushed against Jannika's arm. Goose bumps ran up her arm, right to the top of her head, making her scalp tingle. Jannika moved her arm but couldn't take her eyes off Lee.

"Jannika Peterson, would you like to have lunch with me tomorrow?" Lee said.

Jannika felt like a deer caught in the headlights and was sure her reaction was obvious to Lee.

Lee shifted her plate to one hand and touched Jannika's forearm. "I'd love to hear about how you came to run this fantastic bookstore."

Before Jannika could answer, Paula of the Two Peas was in front of her, taking her plate away.

"Time to clean up, or we're never going to have time to talk about the book," she said.

She took Lee's plate too. Pris came right along behind her, grabbed plates, and took them back to the food table.

The book discussion went on a little longer than usual. Jannika was usually the timekeeper and helped keep the group on track when they went off on a tangent. But tonight, all she was aware of was Leslie sitting next to her. *Lee*, she reminded herself. Memories of that summer long ago rubbed up against the very real presence of this beautiful woman, whose every movement caused a physical reaction in Jannika's body.

Leslie and Patty had been the counselors for Ash and Hemlock cabins. It was Jannika's fifth year at Camp Pine Knoll and her second year as a counselor-in-training. Each summer there were a few new counselors, but most of the counselors returned each year. Leslie was new to this Girl Scout camp, but had worked as a camp counselor for the previous four years.

She'd had an on-again, off-again high school girlfriend. They were off again that summer before her senior year. Leslie was everything Jannika felt she wasn't. Strong, self-assured, smart, calm, and happy. On top of that, Jannika thought she was the most beautiful woman she had ever seen, and the sexiest too. She would offer to do extra chores to be near her. She would crouch behind a pine tree at night to watch Leslie at the campfire with the other counselors and pretend that she was sitting next to her. Oh, she fell hard. Crush was the perfect term, she thought. Because that was how her heart felt each time she saw Leslie or talked with her. Crushed. And now, eighteen years later, she was here, in her bookstore.

Jannika put both her feet flat on the floor, trying to get some ground. Her breath came faster than normal. Could everyone hear her breathe? She glanced around the room and purposefully did not look at the beautiful woman to her right. She looked at the wall clock.

"Well, ladies, this has been a great discussion as always, but it's time for me to close up shop," she said. She tried to pretend tonight was like any other book discussion. Focus, she thought. "Next month's book is *Life Mask* by Emma Donoghue."

"You sure were quiet tonight, Nick," Linda said. "Do you feel all right?"

"She's just tired, right? Long week, I'd bet," said Paula.

Pris was right behind Paula and gave Jannika a little wink over her wife's shoulder.

"Yes, it's been a long week." She looked over at the others. They gathered dishes and spoons and put trash into the trash bucket. "Hannah, could you help me put these chairs back?"

"I'll help too," said Paula.

Jannika leaned over and put her hands on the arms of the upholstered chair. She pushed and slid it back to the reading corner and shimmied it near one of the two large windows. When she stood, Paula was right next to her.

"What's the story, morning glory?" Paula asked.

"About what?" Jannika said. She looked away.

"You'd have to be blind not to see you're interested in Lee, but there's more to that story, isn't there?"

"Nothing gets by you and Pris, does it? But not tonight, Paula. I'll give you a call, okay?"

Paula gave Jannika a pat on the shoulder and walked away.

Jannika turned to see another chair sliding toward her. The fat orange upholstered chair stopped. Lee's smiling head popped up from behind it.

Chapter Five

Lee leaned against the back of the orange chair. She wanted to come across casual and hoped Jannika couldn't hear her heartbeat which seemed louder the closer she got to Jannika. She crossed one foot over the other.

"I asked you to lunch and we were interrupted before you could answer. Are you free tomorrow? Noon? I know you have the store to tend to, but could you get away for an hour?"

"Yes, okay. Okay, noon. Where?" Jannika's words sounded clipped and forced.

"How about Lenny's? I went there the other day and thought they had a pretty good fish chowder for New Hampshire, and it's right down the street here." Lee stood and smoothed the front of her jeans with her hands. Any bit of anxiety was gone now that she knew it really was Jannika from camp. It had been replaced by curiosity and an extra-large dose of attraction.

Jannika had been a beautiful young woman eighteen years ago, with high cheekbones inherited from her Swedish ancestors in Maine, long blond hair, and a casual grace unusual for a seventeen-year-old. But now, she was breathtaking. She was tall and walked like a dancer with legs that went from here to Canada. Her short blond hair accentuated her strong jawline and cheekbones, and her piercing blue-green eyes hadn't changed in eighteen years—they still took her breath away. Lee wanted to get to know this grown-up version of the girl she never forgot from one summer at Camp Pine Knoll.

Jannika rubbed the back of her neck. "Sounds good. Lenny's."

Lee smiled. "I can't wait to find out what your favorite seafood is. See you tomorrow." Well, that sounded pretty weak. Best to make her exit before she lost whatever cool she had. She turned from Jannika and called out, "Good night ladies," to the women who were scattered around the store.

"Nice to meet you."

"See you again."

"Glad Hannah brought you over."

She passed Hannah on her way out the store and gave her a hug.

Hannah whispered in her ear, "Why didn't you tell me you know Jannika? I want the scoop asap."

"Long story, my friend, another time." Lee kissed her on the cheek and walked out.

Jannika watched Lee walk down the third aisle to the front of the store. She walked in the sure-footed stride of someone who knew who they were and where they fit in the world. It was Leslie in the flesh. Here in Grangeton, New Hampshire, of all places after eighteen years.

"As they used to say, take a picture, my friend, it lasts longer," Vicki said, standing at Jannika's side with Linda. "I can't believe I caught our Nick looking at a woman with lust-filled eyes. I think this is a first since I've known you."

The women gathered around her and peppered her with questions. They were protective of her and treated her broken heart with care but also wanted to see her live her life into the future and not be stuck in the past. They thought she was either too afraid to move forward, or she still harbored a fantasy of getting back together with her ex, Joanne-from-Maine, as her friends called her.

Jannika looked around the circle of women and saw love. Paula and Pris were the uber-lesbian-moms of the group and were the most protective of all. Outspoken Vicki and Linda, whose gentle strength balanced Vicki's wildness, and Hannah the romantic, who was a friend of Leslie's. Nina and Lauren were the only ones missing tonight. This was Jannika's extended family here in New Hampshire, along with Marcy, Sarah, her Aunt Gunnie, and her sort-of-adopted Polish grandmother from the bakery three doors down from the bookstore. Now that Lee was no longer in the room, Jannika began to feel more like herself.

"Yes, she is very attractive. Yes, I met her a long time ago. No, she's not an ex. No, we didn't have a *thing*. It was a long time ago and I was surprised to see her again. Yes, I knew her in Maine," Jannika said.

She tried to clear her head while the other women gathered up their coats and dishes, but her body's hum of desire distracted her, and all she could see in her mind was Lee leaning on that big orange chair and smiling at her. Jannika could try to fool her friends, but she knew her flushed face gave her away.

Jannika blew out a sigh of relief when the questions stopped. She hugged each woman good night and closed the bookstore. She needed to talk to Marcy.

Are you around? she texted. Jannika paced in front of her desk, watching her phone for an answer.

Sure thing, what's up? Marcy replied.

Too late to come over?

You okay? Marcy wrote.

Yes. But need to talk. An hour? My house? Jannika's fingers flew over her phone.

You got it. See you then.

Jannika finished her walk around the bookstore, shut off lights, and propped a book here and there.

"Good night, little bookstore." Jannika closed the door behind her.

The streets were dark. Jannika's little car sped out of Grangeton, toward Fairfield. She reached down for her travel mug and noticed a pair of shining eyes a dozen feet ahead. She threw her cup down onto the floor of the passenger's side, grabbed the steering wheel, then veered and braked in time to avoid a lumbering raccoon in the middle of the road. Jannika slowed the car and pulled over onto the gravel edge. She gulped air into her lungs.

"Breathe, Jannika. Breathe." She flipped her blinker and pulled back out onto the road. She took a right, some more deep breaths, and drove down her street. Marcy's car was parked at the end of Jannika's driveway.

"Oh, thank you, Marcy," Jannika said. She pulled in next to Marcy's car.

"Hey you, you okay? You look a little shaky, girl. Let me take one of your bags." Marcy held out a hand.

"A close encounter with a raccoon. Everyone survived," Jannika said.

"You're a little zippy with that car, Jannika. And you know, it's bow-hunting season—that could have been a deer." Marcy's forehead wrinkled with concern.

Jannika unlocked the door to the cottage and flipped on the lights.

"I know, I know—put that down over there." Jannika pointed to a wooden bench inside the door of the cottage.

Jannika flung herself down onto the couch and put her head in her hands. She groaned then sat up.

"Marce, you aren't going to believe this. *I* don't believe it. Did Vicki tell you anything about the woman Hannah was bringing to the book group tonight?"

"Vicki's group, your group? No, why?" Marcy sat on the wicker chair opposite the couch.

Jannika sat back and leaned her head against the cushions. She tapped her fingertips on her thighs. She leaned forward toward Marcy. "I know the new person, Lee. Well, I used to know her."

"Why are you whispering? Is she here?"

Jannika slapped the palms of her hands on her thighs. "No, c'mon, this is serious."

"From where? From Maine? Is that why you're upset? Does she know Joanne?" Marcy asked.

"From Girl Scout camp."

"The Girl Scout camp where you were tortured with crafts?" Marcy smiled.

Jannika smiled back. "Yes. That camp. Aunt Gunnie and Uncle Charlie paid for it every year. The summer after my junior year of high school, I'd broken up with my first girlfriend again. I didn't want to go to camp. I wanted to stay home in my room with my books and write tortured love poems. But Aunt Gunnie made me go. I was a C.I.T., a counselor-in-training, and my cabin camp counselors were Leslie and Patty. Now remember, I'm seventeen and all raging hormones and everything. Leslie was the most beautiful woman I had ever seen. She was kind and patient and…"

"Oh my God, you had a crush on her, didn't you? *She* was at the book group? Shazam! But I don't get why you're so upset," Marcy said.

Jannika bit her lip and fiddled with her left earring.

"It wasn't a little crush. I followed her around everywhere. I wrote secret love letters to her. I think I might have even given her one when I left camp that summer. Oh, it's even worse than I thought." Jannika closed her eyes and groaned.

"You're embarrassed? You were a kid. Did you tell her you remembered her? She probably thought you were very sweet. Sorry, Nick, but I'm not getting it. I see you're upset. You don't have anything to be embarrassed about."

"I was physically attracted to her. I would watch her and Patty carry the canoes down to the lake, and my heart would go nuts. I'd daydream about her falling in love with me. I wanted to know what it would be like to kiss her. I thought about her for months after I was back home. And to be honest…Now don't laugh. She was my go-to fantasy woman, if you know what I mean," Jannika said. Heat rose in her face.

"I won't laugh, and ooh-la-la. You're not seventeen anymore, Nick. You could have one of the ultimate lesbian fantasies plopped in your lap. So to speak." Marcy grinned. "Go for it. You should definitely go for it. Do it for all the lesbians who never could."

"Very funny, Marce."

Marcy crossed the room and sat on the couch next to her.

"I was serious. And for the record, I love hearing you talk about how hot you are for someone. When are you going to see her again? You *are* going to see her again."

"She wants to go to lunch at Lenny's tomorrow to catch up."

"You're going, right?"

"Yes, I'm going. She's gorgeous. Not just beautiful. Gorgeous. And she was so patient and kind to me at camp. She listened to me talk about my mother and how I wanted to find my father. But she probably looks at me like I'm still the seventeen-year-old camper who followed her everywhere."

"Are you really serious? I can say this 'cause we're sister-friends. That voice is little old you trying to protect yourself. No one can look at you and think of a high school kid. Go to lunch. Be your wonderful self. See where it goes. And I, for one, hope it leads right to your bedroom." Marcy snapped her fingers. "Oh yeah."

By the time Jannika told Marcy all the other details of Girl Scout camp and the book group, it was after midnight and two cups of cocoa. Guess they were having a sleepover. Jannika tossed Marcy a pillow and a blanket and wished her a good night.

Jannika closed her bedroom door, took off her clothes and slid into bed. She turned from one side to the other. She tried to think only about Lee, not the Leslie she remembered from back then, the Leslie she'd thought about even when she was with Joanne. The Leslie with those eyes that welcomed her, and those hands that carried canoes, whittled small animals with precision and care, and patted trees as she walked by them.

She wanted to put that young woman aside and think only about the Lee who'd walked into her bookstore. This Lee who smiled, said *Yes, it's me* from across the room tonight, and scooped potato salad on her plate. The Lee whose arm brushed against hers. The Lee who had grown into a beauty as deep and lovely as her beloved mountains in Maine. She needed to put all of that high school crush stuff behind her and just take Lee as Lee.

Chapter Six

Jannika woke to find Marcy gone and a note under an empty mug on the counter with a tea bag, spoon, and jar of honey next to it.

> *Hey kiddo,*
> *I'm in CT the rest of the week, visiting BBs. I may also be seeing the lovely Amy again. If it feels good...*
> *M.*

She made an egg sandwich and ate it in the car on the way to work. The first time she'd eaten an egg sandwich was at Camp Pine Knoll. One of the girls in her cabin—Chrissy? Missy?—put her fried egg between the two halves of her English muffin. Jannika remembered watching Leslie, now Lee, eat her breakfast and wanting to kiss those lips more than anything she had ever wanted in her seventeen years. Jannika ate the last bite of her sandwich and hoped she didn't make a fool of herself at lunch today with Lee.

She wasn't sure why she was worried about that because Lee was one of the few people Jannika had never felt foolish or self-conscious around. She remembered the day after family day at camp, she'd been sitting on the dock, wishing she was like the rest of the girls in her cabin. They had mothers and fathers who came to camp, took pictures, and played field games. Aunt

Gunnie and Uncle Charlie came to camp and they took pictures and Jannika loved them so much, but they weren't her parents. Her mother thought camp was a waste of money, and she had no father. That wasn't exactly correct—she didn't know whether he was dead or alive. He'd left when she was a baby, and the subject was closed with her mother. Every time Jannika asked about her father her mother said, *He's a loser. I'm not talking about it. He left and never looked back.*

But on that long-ago day, Lee had appeared on the dock next to her and sat down. Jannika couldn't remember what she said to Lee about family day, but she remembered being held by Lee's eyes. When Lee listened to her stories, she felt like the most important person in the world. She did remember breaking down and crying because Lee's kindness pierced through the tough girl front she'd shown the rest of the world. She never forgot what that kindness felt like and how it released and nurtured her confidence in herself.

She parked her car behind the store and looked at the back door of the building. She told herself she wasn't going to think about how, in a few hours, she'd be sitting across the table from the woman she's thought about, dreamed about, and fantasized about for the last eighteen years.

As the day passed, Jannika watched the hands on the bookstore clock again and again. Tuesdays were usually slow and today was no exception. She took out her cell phone and compared it to the wall clock more than once.

Sarah breezed in at about ten thirty with a couple of paper bags of children's books that a friend had given her. The children's and young adult books were Sarah's love, and Jannika was happy to hand that part of the job over to her.

"I'm going to be in my nook with the books. Unless you'd like to see them first?"

"We've priced together enough times now, you go ahead and have at it," Jannika said.

She worked on her inventory spreadsheet and pulled up her wanted list to add a few titles to look for this upcoming weekend. Excel was not one of Jannika's skills, and she had to google more than a few *How do I do the thing in Excel?* questions. Anything to keep her mind busy.

When her back muscles grew stiff from the stress of looking at numbers, she turned off the computer and got out a legal pad and pen. She wrote lists for the rest of the morning. She wrote a list of to-do jobs around the cottage, tasks for Sarah to do while she was away next weekend, and a Christmas gift list, and found a grocery app that linked to her store and made a list on that, linking it to recipes that she would probably never make.

She looked up from her lists to give her eyes a break. She liked the look of the new coffee area at the front of the store and the comfy chairs over by the windows in the back. It was a good place for parents to sit and keep an eye on their kids. Jannika glanced at the clock again and her stomach fluttered. It was time to go meet Lee.

"Sarah, I'm going out for lunch today. I'll be back in about an hour. Do you want anything?"

"Hmm. No. I'm trying to be more mindful of eating, so I checked in with my body and it's okay foodwise." Sarah tapped her stomach area with two fingers.

"Sure thing. Be back soon." Jannika made her way to the sidewalk outside the bookstore.

The fall air smelled like warm autumn leaves, wood smoke, and a hint of cinnamon from Bronislaw's Bakery. She'd fantasized about this woman for years, but her crush was not real life, she reminded herself. She figured she'd go and have a conversation and get to know Lee—the real person—and that would put things in perspective. She tried to convince her sweaty palms and jumpy stomach that she was just having a reaction to her past come to life. She pulled open the door to the restaurant and scanned the faces of people in the entryway waiting to be seated.

Jannika didn't see Lee. Ha. After all her worrying, Lee'd probably reconsidered and decided not to come.

She felt someone touch the back of her arm.

"Sorry, I had to take a quick call outside. Hi." Lee smiled a bright, warm smile.

"Hi." Jannika's voice came out in a croak. Her mouth was dry and she licked her lips. She noticed Lee glance at her lips and her knees went a little wobbly.

"I came a little early, because I knew they'd be busy at lunchtime," Lee said.

The entryway was crowded, so she and Lee had no choice but to stand close to each other. Jannika's heart rate picked up speed. She kept her hands in her jacket pockets to keep from fidgeting. Jannika couldn't remember ever feeling this attracted to anyone else. It went beyond physical attraction, way beyond crush. It had been one thing to dream about meeting Leslie again, another to be with her.

But she was afraid they might both be very different now than the people they remembered. She was afraid she might disappoint Lee. And she was also afraid that everything she felt when she was seventeen was still there, and she had no idea what that meant. Her stomach tightened and she swallowed hard. Lee had seemed to be flirting with her at the book group last night. What if Lee was interested in her? That thought scared the hell out of her. God, she felt like she was seventeen again, and not in a good way. Her gaze darted around the room looking for a way out.

"Lee, for two?" the hostess called out.

"Right here."

Jannika followed Lee to the table. They took their seats as the waitress poured water and set down a bread basket.

"What brought you into my bookstore?" Jannika blurted out, surprised at her own words.

Lee took a sip of water. Her eyes didn't leave Jannika's. "A few days after I moved to Fairfield—"

"You live in Fairfield?"

"Yes, I'm renting a house over there. Nice little town. Grangeton's a little too...residential for my taste. Sorry, you probably live here. It's not me."

"I live in Fairfield too. I rent a little carriage house on Myrtle Street off Main Street," she said.

"Funny, Hannah didn't tell me that. I checked out a house a buddy of mine owns in Fairfield, and it felt right. Grangeton seems like the big city to me with all the stores and restaurants. I like farmland and forest. Fairfield has both."

"What *did* Hannah tell you?" Jannika took a sip of water. Her throat was as dry as a cracker.

They were interrupted by the arrival of their waitress. "Hi. I'm Andrea, are you ladies ready to order?"

Jannika ordered a clam roll. Lee glanced at the menu and said, "I'll have what she's having." When the waitress was out of sight, Lee put her forearms on the red Formica tabletop and leaned forward toward Jannika.

"Hannah said I needed to drop by The Pageturner, a fabulous bookstore in Grangeton, run by a gorgeous tall blond goddess by the name of Jannika, who had also come down from Maine. And she said most of the women in town, straight and lesbian, and some of the men had at least a little crush on her," Lee said.

Jannika felt her face grow warm. She shook her head. "Oh boy, I don't think so."

"I was curious. I had only met one other Jannika many years ago, and I wanted to find out if it was the same Jannika and say hello. I was going to stop by the store one day, but Hannah told me about the book group, and I thought, what the heck, it might be a good way to meet folks in town. I stayed up all night so I could finish the book, and then I couldn't think of anything to say."

"As it happens, the book group's not such a great way to meet people from town. None of them are from Grangeton or Fairfield," Jannika said with a smile.

"You are." Lee looked straight into her eyes.

The waitress placed their drinks and two straws on the table. Lee took her straw and unwrapped it slowly. Jannika could not take her eyes off Lee's fingers manipulating the paper wrapper of the straw, as she tore it around and around. She grabbed her own straw and ripped off the paper wrapper.

"I guess you showed that straw." Lee laughed.

Jannika looked at her and laughed too. Their laughter melted some of the tension.

The waitress came and placed their clam rolls and extra napkins on the table.

Time to bring their conversation to the present. "Last night you said you're a park ranger?" Jannika asked.

"I used to be a park ranger in Maine. I was an interpreter. But now I'm a park manager. Rangers in Maine are law enforcement officers. I had a skiing accident a couple of years ago and had to admit to myself that I couldn't ask my body to do certain things out in the field anymore. And if I can't trust my body, I'm not a good ranger. I decided to work as a park interpreter and manager and focus on the people side of the park."

"Were you hurt badly?" Jannika's fingers played with her napkin. Was this question too personal?

"I fell, twisted my leg, and tore my ACL. The surgery went well, but it was a bad tear and I don't like the way my knees feel on skis anymore. Cross-country skiing came with the job in Maine."

"And what do you interpret at the state park? Is that a silly question?" God, it was a silly question.

Lee smiled. "It's not a silly question. A park interpreter tells stories about the history or the wildlife or ecology of the park. We try to gauge the personality of the group we're talking to and fit the stories to the group. Being a good interpreter is an art, really. It helps visitors appreciate and support our state parks and other wild areas."

"It sounds like you love your job like I love mine. Your family's still in Maine?"

"Generations of them. My dad worked for the paper mill in Rumford and retired a few years ago. He and my mom live on my grandfather's farm now. When I was a little girl, my dad would bring home bundles of new paper. It was a few years before I realized that most people bought paper at a store. I loved the smell of that clean, new paper. I used to sketch things I wanted to make or build—my dad made me a corkboard idea wall so I could display my designs."

They continued to talk about Lee's job, their mutual love of the outdoors, and the differences between Maine and New Hampshire.

"I'm so sorry about your knee. So you're like the goodwill ambassadress for state parks."

"Ambassadress?" Lee raised an eyebrow. "I've never been called that. Sounds a bit like what I would have worn to the prom, if I went to the prom." She laughed and Jannika laughed with her. "The bright side is, I took up snowshoeing in place of skiing. And I love it. Have you ever tried?"

"Once, when I was little. I wasn't very good at it. The big tails kept crossing behind me and I'd trip." She demonstrated by putting one index finger over the other.

"Oh, were those the old wooden snowshoes? You should try the new ones. Bean's has some great lightweight shoes. If you ever want to try again, let me know. Great fun and great workout for your ass."

Jannika pictured Lee leaving the bookstore last night. Her face grew hot. *Thanks a lot for my complexion, Swedish ancestors.*

"I'd love to know what you're thinking about right now," Lee said. She finished the last bit of her clam roll, wiped her mouth and hands with her napkin, and grinned. "That was great. Kind of messy"—she looked down at the bits of food on her plate and paper placemat—"but great." She looked back up at Jannika. "So…"

Jannika watched every movement she made. Part of her couldn't believe she was sitting across from Leslie after all these years.

"Haddock."

"Haddock?" Lee asked.

"You wanted to know my favorite seafood. The other night when you asked me to lunch. What's yours, and what was the name of the state park you're at?"

"You're changing the subject."

"Yes, I am," Jannika said, leaning back in the booth. She needed to get her mind off Lee's beautiful backside and concentrate on conversation. If she focused on the conversation she would be okay, but if she let the reality of Lee sitting across from her come into focus, she was afraid she might start squirming in her seat. As it was, she didn't know where it was safe to look. If she watched Lee's hands, she thought about what her hands might feel like touching her. If she looked at her face, part of her wanted to climb onto the table and kiss her. She tried to vary where her gaze traveled. Lee probably thought she looked like she had some eye problem, so she stopped doing the eye shifting thing.

"I really do want to know about your job and your park." Jannika hoped she looked like a normal person.

"It's scallops and Watt's Lake State Park. The park is about thirty minutes from here, south, near Kingston. I was a park manager for the past year while I was on light duty in Maine. But it was a temporary position and I wanted a smaller park with camping. Have you ever been there?"

"No, I haven't camped since..." Jannika said.

"Since Camp Pine Knoll? I'll take you over to my park sometime if you'd like. Now, what about you? I remember you brought an armload of books with you when you came to camp. Have you always managed bookstores?"

"I worked part time in a Barnes and Noble and got a job in a small used and rare book store during college. After I graduated I took a position as a community business manager for the Barnes and Noble in Portland. I didn't like it. I was too removed from the books. Then I worked weekends in the local library, went back to the little bookstore, and bought and sold used books online," Jannika said.

"I hear the passion in your voice when you talk about books. But I can't believe you moved away from Stillmeadow. I remember you said you loved the mountains."

"I missed my mountains but I needed to get away from my mother. I moved away as fast as I could. I went to a local community college near Stillmeadow and finished college over at USM in Portland. My mother didn't want me to finish college over in Portland. She had a thing about Portland—I guess it had bad memories for her. That's where she lived after high school, and where she met the man who was my father. I don't know if you remember that story," Jannika said.

"I remember more than you probably think I do." Lee leaned forward.

Jannika felt the heat climb up her cheeks. She couldn't remember blushing this much since grade school. She smiled. "Oh, do you?" she said.

"You'd be surprised," Lee answered. "You seemed very happy at camp for the most part."

"I loved camp. Certain years were better than others." Jannika looked straight into Lee's eyes.

"For me as well," Lee said. Her eyes never left Jannika's. "You were an industrious girl as I remember—you always wanted to help Patty and me."

"Industrious? Lee...I..." Jannika looked down at her hands. She was flirting and having fun with Lee and had been on the verge of talking about her teenage crush. Talk about oversharing. She didn't know Lee really at all. And her old crush looked a bit dated and silly now that she sat across from the real Lee and not her fantasy Leslie. She didn't want to make a fool out of herself.

She took a sip of water. She watched Lee take a sip of water. She looked around the restaurant.

"Do you know what time it is? I should be getting back."

"Jannika, the last thing I wanted to do was make you uncomfortable, and I have." Lee said.

"No, you haven't made me uncomfortable. A lot of time has gone by between that summer and now."

The waitress slipped the check onto the table as she walked by. Jannika and Lee reached for it at the same time. They looked up and locked eyes.

"I'll get it," said Lee reaching into her back pocket.

"No, that's okay, I—"

"I've got it, Jannika," Lee said, placing cash with the check on the end of their table. "I invited you."

The authority in Lee's voice made Jannika's stomach do a flip and her head feel light. She tried to distract herself from her body's reactions. Lee reached across the table and covered Jannika's hand with hers. A wave of warmth moved up her arm and down her spine. She stared at Lee and wanted to stop, but she couldn't take her eyes away from Lee's.

She heard Lee's voice saying something and refocused.

"…for taking time out of your day to go to lunch with me. I felt really welcomed at the book group last night. They seem like a special group of women. I hope they'll have me back. We didn't get a chance to talk about your bookstore."

As Lee spoke, Jannika caught a glimpse of something behind her lovely eyes. Something she wanted to know. Warmth rose in her body like mercury in a thermometer. She was fascinated by Lee's mouth and the way it formed words. She couldn't stop looking at her mouth.

Lee pulled her hand away and leaned back in the booth. That broke the spell. "Can I take you to dinner this weekend if you don't have other plans already?"

Jannika tried to place the words *this weekend* into some kind of context in her brain. October. Weekend. Today was Tuesday. Oh, right, the Simon's weekend was this weekend.

"I'm busy this weekend," Jannika said. Her mind was busy and her legs felt like cooked spaghetti. How could this woman be more good-looking than she remembered? And she was definitely more sexy. Of course, they said women were sexiest in their forties, and she agreed. Whoa. She had no idea what she was doing or feeling, and she didn't want things to get out of control. Okay, more out of control. Jeez.

Jannika scooted out of the booth. "Anyway, I've got to get back to the bookstore." Her voice came out clipped and short, even though she really did need to get back. She tried to ignore the familiar feeling of anxiety whenever emotions got too close.

"Oh, okay," Lee said. She sounded a little hurt, and that brought Jannika up short.

"I'm not putting you off," she said gently. "I have a book thing this weekend. Every spring and fall I go to North Adams to get together with some bookseller friends and pick out books from this place called Simon's Warehouse. Combination of business and pleasure." Somehow talking about books brought her back solidly to the here and now, and she owed now-Lee a confession. "And to be honest, I was a little bit anxious about coming to lunch with you after all these years."

"I was too. Just so you know." Lee rose from the booth. "How about when you get back? A midweek supper at Portsmouth Brewery? Wednesday at seven?"

"Sure," Jannika said over her shoulder as she walked out the door of the restaurant. "And my turn to get the check." Jannika felt better once they were outside, walking around.

"Deal. Okay if I walk back with you? My truck's parked over that way," Lee said.

"I'd like that." She wanted to walk to Boston and back with Lee. She couldn't believe Lee lived right in Fairfield.

"We didn't get dessert. Cookie?" Lee pointed to the doorway of a shop.

The smell of Bronislaw's Bakery wafted out the door and into the street. The smell on cookie days doubled business. A round woman with a stern face was behind the counter.

"Hi, Babcia, this is Lee."

"And I would like to buy this lovely lady a cookie today." Lee gave a short formal bow.

Jannika smiled. "Oatmeal raisin for me."

"And I'll have a black-and-white."

"Just one? You girls are too skinny. Always worried about food—what is good food, what is bad food. Worry makes you sick, not food." She shook her finger at them as she passed them each a cookie wrapped in thin paper. Lee paid for the cookies and opened the door for Jannika.

Lee bit into her cookie. "This is incredible. What did you call her? Baba?"

"Babcia. It's Polish for grandmother. That's what everyone calls her. She's sort of my stand-in grandmother here in town. She brought me soup and bread when I first moved here. Her son helped me move some bookcases at the store and at the cottage. She reminds me of my grandmother, my mormor. Like these cookies. Crisp on the outside, all soft on the inside."

"I feel a little plain having a grandma and grampie."

"There's nothing plain about you, Lee." Jannika couldn't believe that came out of her mouth.

Lee smiled at her and the street disappeared beneath her feet.

They turned down a narrow cobblestone side street leading to the employees only entrance for the people who lived and worked in the building that housed The Pageturner—an insurance company, a martial arts studio, and several apartments on the third floor. Jannika turned around a few steps from the door.

"Thanks for the cookie," she said. She popped the last bite into her mouth.

All of a sudden she was very aware of her mouth and Lee's mouth and the distance between the two.

"Let me take that," Lee said, pointing to Jannika's balled up piece of cookie paper wrapping.

"Thanks."

Lee took the paper from Jannika's hand and stepped closer. She brushed the outside corner of Jannika's mouth with her thumb.

"You had a little piece of cookie there," Lee said. Her voice was soft and low.

Jannika looked into Lee's eyes. Her heart raced.

Lee stepped back and ran her hand through her hair.

"Can I call you at the bookstore?" Lee said.

"Yes, please. But I better go now, so my assistant can have a break," Jannika said. She grabbed the cold metal railing.

"See you." Lee waved and smiled back at Jannika.

Jannika's heart banged in her chest. She sat down on the steps and watched Lee round the corner and toss the ball of paper into the trash can. Her head felt light as a balloon. She rubbed her sweaty palms on the front of her pants and rose to face the afternoon.

Chapter Seven

Lee hopped into her Toyota pickup and let out a long sigh. Jannika was even more beautiful in the October sun than last night at the bookstore. Hannah had described her well, but nothing could have prepared her for this grown-up version of the girl she'd once known. She looked like some kind of Nordic queen. And she would bet that Jannika had no idea the effect she had on other women.

She knew she had pushed things a bit, brushing the cookie crumbs off her lip, but she loved Jannika's reaction. If she'd thought she wanted to kiss her last night, that was nothing compared to this afternoon. Her body flushed with warmth and she felt a tingle deep in her belly. She was surprised at her reaction. No one had caused her to react this way in a long time.

She'd had a couple of brief relationships since her wife Shannon's death five years ago, and they'd both run their course and fizzled out. She remained friends with both women. But she hadn't met anyone who had this effect on her. When she'd walked in with Hannah last night and seen Jannika laughing with her friends, the scene had narrowed and compressed until there'd been only Jannika. And her remembered image of Jannika at seventeen changed and morphed into Jannika at thirty-four.

Lee was a steady person. *Slow rivers run deep*, her mother always said. But in that moment, seeing Jannika for the first time in eighteen years, she'd had the urge to run over, scoop her in her arms, and kiss her until tomorrow. This new desire for Jannika the adult woman was a bonfire on a summer night. It wasn't just the physical attraction, and it wasn't just the memory of that summer at camp. She felt like they knew each other. Lee hadn't formed any deep connections with anyone, friends or lovers, since Shannon's death. She didn't want that kind of connection anymore. It was easier to live without the risk of losing someone again. But part of her wanted to walk toward Jannika, and part of her wanted to run into the forest where she felt safe.

She thought about that summer at camp. The group from Jannika's cabin was always the first at the dining lodge for breakfast, and Lee had breakfast duty every day that summer. Jannika would take her time as she moved down the line, shoulders back, a hand on one hip and the other hand on the food counter. She would hold up the line asking Lee questions. *Are you and Patty taking us out on the lake today? If it rains, will you be at the arts and crafts cottage?*

Canoe trips were usually four to a canoe, but that July day there were three in Lee's canoe. Lee took the rear so she could navigate, Jannika was in the middle, and another cabin leader was in the front. Sandy? Sally? Lee couldn't remember. She did remember the curve of Jannika's back and the tanned skin that peeked out below her life vest as the canoe moved across the water. After a few minutes on the lake, Jannika moved her long legs carefully and she turned around to sit facing Lee.

"You know, I almost have my Paddle, Pole, and Roll patch." Jannika fiddled with the zipper on the front of her life vest.

Lee tried not to look at Jannika's chest. She tried to repeat the rule about getting involved with campers to herself. The orientation for counselors lasted a week before the campers arrived, and the woman who hired them had everyone line up in the dining hall at the end of their training week as she spoke. "These girls are all raging hormones. They will cry. They will try to cajole you to call their parents, or get extra food for them, or other privileges. Sometimes a teenage girl will get a harmless crush on her counselor. Because you are role models. Do not under any circumstances encourage their behavior. You will be let go and you will not get a recommendation from this camp. This is the Girl Scouts of America."

"I have two things left to do for my patch." Jannika lowered the zipper on her life vest.

Lee reminded her to keep her vest on.

Jannika zipped it up, then down again slowly as she spoke. "I have to demonstrate how to choose a PFD that fits right." Her vest was almost completely unzipped and she turned and looked at her side. "You see these side thingies?"

Lee's eyes were not on the life vest.

Sandy/Sally yelled, "Yo, Leslie. Are we going in a circle for a reason?"

Jannika spun back into place, facing away from her again. She tried to focus on paddling and steering the canoe. Jannika looked over her shoulder at her. Her eyes were beautiful. Full of daring and mischief. "Want to know what the second thing is that I need for my patch?" She leaned forward and said something to Sandy/Sally. "Role-play a safety situation!" Jannika yelled as she slipped out of her life vest, grabbed the side of the canoe, leaned over, and rolled them all. She knew Jannika was a strong swimmer. She knew it was role-play. But when she heard her yell for help, her training took over and she swam quickly to Jannika's side. She wrapped one arm under her arms and around her chest and treaded water.

"You okay?" Lee yelled to Sandy/Sally who was swimming the canoe in their direction.

"Yup."

Jannika leaned her head back against Lee's chest. "I'm also supposed to show you how comfortable I am in the water." Jannika's hand caught Lee's pumping leg and slid up the inside of her left thigh.

"Hey." Lee released Jannika, who slid under but popped to the surface and swam quickly to Sandy/Sally and the canoe. All three of them swam the canoe to shore with two more camp canoes catching up and accompanying them. As they pulled the canoe to shore, Jannika said in a low voice, "Cover for me? Please. I'm sorry." Jannika's face was bright red.

Lee had replayed that sequence of events more times in the past eighteen years than she would ever admit to anyone.

Lee had caught only glimpses of that bold, playful Jannika at lunch today. She'd watched Jannika's body language and tone go from playful and open to businesslike, then neutral, and back again. Part of Lee's job as a ranger was to assess her surroundings. It was second nature to her. She was so good at it, she used to train new hires. Her surroundings included people. Last night and today, that included Jannika.

What she saw was a woman who, for whatever reason, did not trust herself.

Lee reached into the dashboard cubby for a hair tie, pulled back her hair into a ponytail, put on her ball cap, and drove toward home. She needed a good long hike. The trail she'd found near her new home was perfect. She did her best thinking in the woods.

There was something about Jannika under that near-perfect exterior that was both mysterious and tender. She wanted to learn more about her. She wanted to know her fears, what gave her delight, what ticked her off, what she liked, and what she didn't like. Lee thought about the people who had hurt Jannika and made wounds so deep, she couldn't or wouldn't trust her feelings. A bubble of anger rose in her throat.

CHAPTER EIGHT

Jannika picked up the rental van bright and early Friday and sent Sarah one more text. Sarah reassured her for the fifth time that Jannika had left her in charge before and all would be well. She also added that this was a great time for a trip because she noticed Jannika's aura was a little cloudy lately. The morning air was crisp and smelled a bit of overripe apples and wood smoke. Jannika looked at the gold-leafed birch trees behind the cottage, exploding with color against the bright blue sky.

She took this trip twice a year, once in the spring and once in the fall. Excitement fluttered in her stomach. Simon's Warehouse was a gigantic building full of books, mostly remainders from publishers and some overstocks from bookstore chains. She'd found some fabulous reads there this past year to bring back to The Pageturner. One of the best parts of her job was introducing her customers to some wonderful authors who weren't on the *New York Times* bestseller list.

The bookseller open house weekend at Simon's couldn't have come at a better time, Jannika thought, as she pulled the rental van on to I-95 south. This weekend would give her time to think and time to spend with book people. She usually met up with Edgar, the bookseller she'd worked for while she was in college. He bought and sold rare books and also sold popular books in an online store. They never planned where or when they would meet during the weekend. Edgar liked to leave things to chance. Edgar had been her boss, then her mentor, and now he was her friend.

The drive to the Berkshires in Western Massachusetts was golden, with splotches of red and russet brown along the route. The beauty of the trees was more than visual—it made its way through her body. Her spine lengthened as the muscles in her back relaxed. She pulled off in Littleton to stop for lunch at a place once recommended to her by the town's librarian. Edgar had told her once that when he traveled, he called the local librarian in whatever town he was going to and asked them for recommendations. The smell of peppers and onions on the grill greeted her at the door, and the face of a friend was the first thing she noticed when she walked in. Edgar. She shook her head and smiled as he waved her over to the end booth near the side door.

"Jannika Peterson, fancy meeting you here." Edgar stood as she approached the booth.

Jannika leaned over the table and gave Edgar a quick hug. She was always surprised by what Aunt Gunnie would call the *delightful* amount of aftershave he used. She hoped the bathroom had soap, so she could wash her face and neck before getting back into her car. The smell would be tough to endure for two hours on the road until she made it to the bed-and-breakfast in North Adams. They both settled into the booth. Edgar waved a couple of fingers at the waitress and asked her for a menu for Jannika.

"You taught me well," Jannika said.

"The librarian trick?"

"Of course. They've never let me down."

"They always know the best places to eat, don't they? Luscious librarians, all. I haven't met one I didn't fall a little in love with," Edgar said. He adjusted his half-frame glasses. "How is your store? I'm sorry I didn't see you in the spring. Helen had a hip replacement and it was a spousal sacrifice to stay with my wife after hip surgery and miss Simon's weekend."

"I know you're joking," Jannika said.

"A little joke, a little truth," Edgar said. "Are things good at the store? I heard you've been newsworthy in New Hampshire."

The waitress brought Jannika water and took her order. When she left, Jannika pointed to the lone roll in the red plastic bread basket on the table. Edgar nodded, and she took the soft round roll and split it open.

"Give me a second, I'm starving. Tell me how is Helen?" Jannika tossed her napkin in her lap and took a bite of bread.

"She's fine. Good as new. Wants me to hike with her, silly woman. We've been married over thirty years and we've never hiked. I'm not fond of fresh air and all that. She says I spend too much time at the shop."

Jannika stopped chewing and looked at Edgar.

"I know I do, but I always have, and if I haven't changed in thirty years, I'm probably not going to." Edgar placed the palms of his hands flat on the table.

"Change can be good, Edgar. I think I remember you saying that to me, once upon a time," Jannika said.

"Yes, but you're young, and as much as I miss working with you and visiting with you, you were ready to have your own bookstore. And you have to admit, the offer came at just the right time. Billingsworth, was it? Does he appreciate the attention the store is getting from the papers?"

"Bosworth. He keeps mentioning that the store is tying him down. He says it with a smile and I don't know him well enough to know if he's joking or not. He likes that sales are up most months. But you know how it is, some months are great and some months we can barely make wages and utilities. It makes me a little nervous."

"Of course, sales are up with you there," Edgar said.

"Thanks. He's not at the store much. He brings in some remainders once in a while, or a box from a library sale, but he pretty much lets me run the store."

The waitress returned with Jannika's meal and asked, "Do you folks want one check or two?" She put Jannika's plate on the table.

Jannika had a mouth full of pepper steak sandwich and motioned to Edgar that she would take care of her own check.

"Glad to see you're enjoyin' your lunch." The waitress pulled out her pad and walked away.

Jannika finished chewing. "Are you after anything in particular this trip?"

"I'm looking for a smidgeon of new fiction, any unusual nonfiction, and interesting cookbooks—people still buy them. I'm very happy the big five are a bit more creative with their covers this year. Remember, it was all feet and shoes for a couple of years. Every cover—empty shoes or half a person, just legs, feet, and shoes. Tedious. This year it's a bit better, but there is a preponderance of curlicue fonts in the titles. Have you noticed?" Edgar asked.

"Yes, I've noticed." Damn, she'd missed Edgar. "I'm sorry I haven't emailed or called in the past year."

"You seem more settled at your store in New Hampshire." He looked at Jannika and touched the back of her hand. "It's a nice thing to see."

"I had no idea how wonderful it would feel to live so close to my Aunt Gunnie. It does make me feel more grounded." She wished she felt that way about other areas of her life. Meeting Lee again was exciting but also so unsettling. And no matter how much she loved The Pageturner, she was just an employee.

"Jannika?"

"Oh, my mind was back at the store," Jannika said. "I've heard some talk around town that Bosworth's the kind of person who gets all excited about a project for a while, then abandons it for some new shiny thing. I guess he bought the local movie theater a few years back but got tired of it. Now it's sitting empty in the middle of town. I was so excited when Aunt Gunnie told me about the job. I jumped on it, but now I'm wishing I'd done a little more research. Edgar, I'm in love with this store. I feel like it's mine. I feel like I'm where I'm supposed to be, and I'm terrified of losing it. I lie awake at night and try to figure out what to do if that happens." This was the first time she'd said anything about losing the store out loud. Putting it out there gave it life somehow, and what had seemed like her mind blowing things out of proportion, now seemed a very real possibility. The place between her shoulder blades tightened and not from the long drive this time.

"Have you talked to Billingsworth?"

"Bosworth."

"Bosworth. You've been there long enough to know what his long-range plan is for the store. I hope he's seen what you do and compensates you for that as well. I suppose you haven't had that conversation, either? It's always better to know than to wonder, my dear."

"I will. When I get back. I'll send him an email."

"Call him."

Jannika scowled at Edgar. "Yes, sir. I'll call him."

"Affirmation applauded. For now, your store is well tended, so enjoy this weekend. We're away from our shops, and we can browse, buy, and talk books all weekend." He clapped his hands and rubbed them back and forth. "You look well, my dear," Edgar said, peering over his glasses. "Here's to serendipitous searches."

Jannika met up with two booksellers she knew from Maine over the weekend and had dinner with them and an older couple from New Hampshire who ran a store in Portsmouth. She kept the young men who loaded boxes of purchased books into vehicles busy all Saturday, and it wasn't until Sunday morning that she had a chance to talk with Edgar again.

"I don't know why I'm still buying—the van is nearly full." Jannika scanned titles of books in boxes on a long table. "I always save this room for last. Good buys this year?" She turned to face Edgar who was also scanning titles.

"I buy most of my books by word of mouth or from dealers online now. I have some lovelies I couldn't say no to, but mostly I come now to talk shop and see how my kinfolk are faring in this treacherous business. Whenever I'm in this room, I remember the first year you accompanied me here. You had done your homework magnificently, but I had to corral your enthusiasm." He placed one hand on a carton of books and tapped his fingers. "They are difficult to resist."

Jannika understood perfectly. "I feel all business in the other rooms. Everything is in cartons and stacked on that big metal shelving. All I have to do is look at my Simon's map and the lists of titles at the end of each row and choose. But here I get to see the covers, touch them, read the blurbs or the first page. When I came here that first time with you I already knew where to go to read reviews, but you taught me the best book buying skills—how to listen to my customers and how to ask the right questions." Jannika pulled a book out of a box. "Like this one. Small independent press—"

"No publicity to speak of." Edgar took another copy of the book from the box and turned it over. "An okay blurb, but nothing to crow about."

"But I heard a great review a while back on a podcast—"

"Wait. A pod...?"

"A podcast. It's like a radio show. You can listen to it on your computer or smartphone. I know, I know, you don't have a smartphone." Jannika remembered when she'd introduced Edgar to the computer she convinced him to buy for his store. He had no interest until he saw Jannika search online for a rare book for a customer. His excitement about the books he could find, and the information he could find about the books, overtook him for a few weeks, and he stayed at the store well after closing. Jannika thought Helen might never forgive her. Despite his digital conversion, he saw no use in a cell phone.

"Nor will I ever."

"Right. But there are a ton of them out there now. About everything. I think this is one modern development that you might actually like, Edgar. I'll email you some links. You can listen on the computer. Anyhow, people are discovering smaller presses this way. Me included. I love being able to give some of these books a second chance. They might not have made a splash in the big bookstores, but I can hand-sell this one like crazy. Face-to-face with my customers."

Jannika loved her customers. She loved The Pageturner. The thought of Joe Bosworth selling the store made her throat ache. Here she was, buying books for the next six months like she was secure in her job. But if she lost her job, she would lose everything. Successful bookstores were becoming rare, and jobs in those bookstores, even more so. Edgar was right. She should have called Joe when she'd first started hearing the rumors.

CHAPTER NINE

Jannika stood in her bedroom next to a pile of shirts and pants on the queen-size bed. Nothing looked right. She didn't want to look like she was coming on to Lee, and she didn't want to look like she was dressed for a business meeting or a funeral either. Her in-between clothes seemed too casual. She tried on a skirt, but it seemed too short. Too much leg. Tonight was the first date since Joanne that she felt excited about. She liked Leslie—Lee. It was the intense, too intense physical attraction that scared her.

She had been very physically attracted to Joanne—that's how their relationship began. They made love the night they met. Sex was their fail-safe method of communicating and Joanne's way of softening her up. If they had a disagreement, they made love. If they had to make a decision, they made love first. They were great in the bedroom, but in the living room, not so much. In a weird way, she already had more with Lee than she'd ever had with Joanne. But would sex ruin it all?

Jannika turned in front of the mirror and shook her head. She was going to enjoy this date. Her favorite black jeans were perfect. They looked great and were comfortable. Her turquoise blouse highlighted her blue-green eyes and brightened her hair.

"Done. Now put yourself in the car and get there," she said.

❖

The Portsmouth Brewery was popular with locals and tourists, not too cozy and not too formal. Lee arrived early and sipped a beer in a high-backed wooden booth. She chose the bench facing the windows and door so she could watch for Jannika. She leaned back against the booth to counteract the tiny butterflies in her belly.

She got up as Jannika approached. She hadn't thought Jannika could look more beautiful than the first time she saw her again at the bookstore. She tried to ignore her jitters but found it hard to believe she was on a date with Jannika, after all these years. Something lightened in her heart every time she looked at her. She held out her hands.

"You look gorgeous. May I?" Lee's heart beat faster as she asked the question. She hoped Jannika wouldn't be put off by her enthusiasm.

Jannika turned around and let Lee help her out of her jacket. Lee hung the jacket next to hers on the black wrought iron hooks attached to the side of the booth.

"You're here early. I thought I'd get here before you."

"Confession. I got here early so I could watch your entrance." Lee smiled and sat down. Was she dorky to admit that? Probably.

Jannika laughed, covered her mouth with her hand, and slid into the booth opposite her.

"Am I missing something?" Yeah, she was dorky.

"No, just nerves. You are…stunning." Jannika's words came out a little too loud and a blush crept up her neck and jawline.

"Thanks." Lee could watch Jannika all day, and she really didn't care if the table next to theirs was probably enjoying their date too. "The waitress already brought menus. I'm hungry. You?" Food was always a safe topic.

"I'm starving. I could probably eat a whole pizza all by myself, but that wouldn't be too attractive on a first date, would it?" Jannika asked.

"No, you'd have to wait until at least the third date before you spring the whole-pizza thing on me." She picked up her menu and looked over it at Jannika. To be honest, she was having a hard time looking at the menu and not at Jannika's eyes, which appeared to match the color of her shirt exactly.

"Oh, so you're betting on a third date, are you?" Jannika smiled.

Jannika seemed to relax every time she smiled. She wanted to see more of that smile. "Hoping, more like...So what's that saying? Penny for your thoughts." She liked this playful side of Jannika. She watched her twirl the top button of her blouse.

"I was thinking—" Jannika said.

"Hi. What looks good to you, ladies?"

All conversation stopped when the server interrupted with his very energetic and cheery welcome. Jannika ordered number four, a small barbecue chicken pizza.

"And I'll have the Hawaiian ten inch," Lee said.

"Do you really like pizza with pineapple on it?" asked Jannika.

"Yes, I do. I love the sweet and tangy pineapple with the salty ham and tomato sauce. You know, I've found that those who mock the Hawaiian pizza have never actually tasted one," she said.

"You're right, I haven't ever tasted one. But just the thought," Jannika said with an exaggerated shudder. She scrunched up her nose and shook her head.

"Maybe I can convince you to try it tonight? I remember you as very adventurous." Lee chuckled as she looked over the top of Jannika's head at a little girl who was standing in the next booth making faces at her.

Jannika patted the top of her blond head. "Is there something wrong with my hair? Is it all sticking up from the wind or something?"

"No, sorry." Lee pointed at the little girl, who ducked back down in the booth. "There's a little girl next door who's been making faces at me." Lee had always liked kids, and the girl reminded her of how much she missed her nieces and nephews in Maine.

"And you've been making faces right back. You were so great with the little kids at camp. Do you get to interact with kids at work now?"

"Not very much. Other park staff do most of the programming, but I get to do some once in a while. But I get plenty of kid time in the winter with my sisters and brothers and their kids."

"Lucky kids, having the number-one camp counselor in Maine as their aunt. Do you have any kids?"

Lee would never get used to talking about Shannon and her death. "I was in a relationship for eight years with a truly wonderful woman named Shannon, and we were about to take that step in our relationship when she died in an accident." She straightened her spine for strength.

"Oh, Lee. I'm so sorry." Jannika's voice dropped.

"She died just over five years ago. I had a couple of girlfriends in my early twenties, and then I met Shannon and fell hard. We had a great relationship. Steady. Solid, you know? Since she died, I've dated some and had a short relationship that ended very amicably. We both came to the realization that we weren't right for each other." Sometimes Lee wasn't sure if anyone would feel right again.

"I'm so sorry. I can't imagine that kind of loss," Jannika said.

"There's part of me that will always miss Shannon." Lee sighed. "It's always tricky talking about your past during a date, isn't it?" She didn't tell Jannika how Shannon died, or that Lee thought it should have been her that the speeding driver hit that day. She could still hear Shannon's voice that day, asking Lee to go to the store for bread and toilet paper. She'd yelled at Shannon, complaining that she always went to the store and couldn't Shannon just get off her backside for once and go. Shannon had slammed the door on her way out. Bread and toilet paper and her pissy attitude cost her Shannon.

Lee had done a lot of grief work over the past five years. She was still working on her need to accommodate people, as if that could make up for the time she didn't accommodate Shannon.

"It all depends what part of your past you're talking about. I once heard about someone's entire psychiatric history and medication list on the first date. *That* was not first date material," Jannika said gently. She had never survived a loss as deep as Lee's, and she wasn't sure what she should say. Lee was looking at her like she hadn't registered what Jannika said, like she was still wrapped in her memories. Jannika unrolled her fork and knife from the paper napkin and adjusted the flatware in front of her on the paper placemat. She felt deep admiration for this woman sitting across from her who'd endured such a deep heartbreak. She thought she could probably learn a lot about healing from her.

"Thanks for telling me," Jannika said. Her voice caught a bit in her throat as she thought about the enormity of Lee's loss. She picked up her water glass and had a sip.

Lee leaned forward and looked deep into Jannika's eyes.

"You're welcome." She leaned back. "I hope that pizza is coming soon. I'm hungrier than I thought," Lee said.

"Me too. They don't give you bread sticks or anything here." Jannika went along with the change in conversation.

"Apparently they don't give you drinks either," Lee joked. "Did that guy go on break maybe?" Lee said. She leaned out of the booth a little to scan the restaurant. Their server must have noticed because thirty seconds later he materialized at their table.

"Yes, ladies. What can I do for you?"

"Could we get something to drink while we're waiting for our pizza?" Lee asked.

"Something on tap? It's totally busy here tonight, and I'm not used to it being so busy during the week. I'm so sorry."

"No worries. I'm going to have another Wicked Wheat. What about you, Jannika?" Lee asked.

"I'll have the Portsmouth Pale Ale," Jannika said. Jannika felt much more comfortable tonight than she had at their lunch. She loved the way Lee had looked at her when she walked to the booth earlier. She swore she could hear her heart beating when she got to the booth and Lee offered to take her jacket.

A young woman came over with their beers, and after a few minutes, the server followed with their pizzas.

"All set?" he asked.

"I'm fine, what about you, Lee?" Jannika asked.

"I am ready for my Hawaiian pizza." Lee waved her hands like she was doing a hula dance, while making some *uh-huh, uh-huh* hip-hop sounds. "Ready for a bite?"

"Oh, I don't know, Lee. It even looks a little weird," Jannika said. Lee's excitement was adorable but the pizza still didn't appeal.

"You know, I think in Hawaii they may put Spam on pizza instead of ham. I think I read that someplace," Lee said.

"You are a font of pizza trivia," Jannika said, lifting a piece of her pizza to her mouth. She curled the edges before she took a bite.

"You can tell a lot about a woman from the way she eats pizza," Lee said.

Jannika chewed and swallowed. "Oh, you can?" She wasn't at all self-conscious now, no, not at all.

"Yes, for instance, some women get right in there and take the flat bite, some—believe it or not—bite from the sides of the piece, and some women, like you, curl the edges of the piece of pizza before they put it in their mouth." Lee took a bite of her pizza.

"And you get right in there," Jannika said with a smile.

"I do indeed. And you, Jannika, like things tidy and neat."

"I think I can get right in there," Jannika said challenging Lee. She liked the way Lee was teasing her.

"Show me," Lee said. She picked up a piece of Hawaiian pizza and held the point of the triangle toward Jannika. She moved it closer to her mouth.

Jannika set her mouth in a line. She took a deep breath. She looked at the pizza. Pizza with pineapple on it. Unnatural. She took another deep breath. Lee withdrew the slice a few inches. "You don't have to," Lee said. "Sorry if I'm being a jerk about this."

Jannika reached over, grabbed the piece of Hawaiian pizza, and took a full flat frontal get-right-in-there bite, then reached for her napkin to wipe her mouth.

"Aha. So you can get in there, but you still like to tidy up afterward," Lee said with a great big smile on her face.

Jannika was smiling and chewing, and chewing. "It's good. No, it is. I tried not to think about what was on top of it and just taste it, and it's good. And," she said with fanfare and a mock bow, "I *can* get in there with the best of them." She finished with her chin raised and what she hoped was a haughty look.

"Now that's something to look forward to," Lee said.

The look that Lee gave her made her ears sting. She watched Lee's glance shift down slightly, then back up to her face. Part of her wanted Lee to know how much she wanted her, and part of her was a little embarrassed that she couldn't control her body's response. Even when she was joking around, Lee looked at her with more than desire. Jannika was afraid that this was all too good to be true, that it was nothing more than the initial excitement of being with Lee and sitting across the table from her after all these years.

They finished their beers, a half pitcher of water, and both pizzas. Jannika was surprised that talking with Lee was so easy. Was it silly to be fascinated to learn what Lee's favorite foods were? She didn't feel silly. Her cheeks hurt from smiling so much at dinner. She wanted to know more. She wanted to know everything about Lee.

CHAPTER TEN

The server arrived with the check, and Jannika claimed it. "This one's mine, remember? And I think I might need to walk some of this pizza off before I go home." Jannika didn't want the date to end at the restaurant. She was so used to dates going downhill fast, but with Lee the time flew and she wanted to ask Lee so many questions. Part of her wanted to jump up and down like the kid in the booth behind her, and she kept reminding herself that this was only their second meal together.

"A walk sounds like a great idea. And thanks for dinner." Jannika was glad Lee didn't argue about the check. "Want to go down by the water?"

"How about around town, Market Square, maybe?" Jannika replied.

Lee stood, took Jannika's leather jacket off the hook, and held it out for her. "Allow me," she said.

"Sure. Thanks," Jannika said. She put her arms into the jacket and her stomach fluttered as Lee's fingers brushed the back of her neck. Lee's attention made her feel cared for and special. She usually shrugged off any offer of chivalrous behavior, finding it stifling, but she softened at the gesture when Lee did it.

The brick sidewalks of Portsmouth were still filled with people on this October night. Most of the shops had closed for the day, but there were a few still open, probably hoping to get a few more tourist dollars before the snowy winter. The side streets were narrow in this historic town, made for carts and horses and not parked cars. Jannika loved looking at the old sea captains' houses and the smaller family capes and saltboxes that sat on the streets right outside the square. She told Lee about the beautiful flower gardens that private home owners opened to the public for three weeks during the summer.

"Hey, look at that," Lee said, pointing up at a large gargoyle perched on the turret of an old Victorian house. "Pretty cool. I wonder how long he's been perched up there?"

"How do you know it's a he?" Jannika asked.

"Well…" Lee raised her eyebrows. "I guess I don't."

"It is actually pretty easy to tell the difference between male and female gargoyles. A male's ears are always more pointed than a female's. The females have more rounded ears." Jannika explained while tracing her finger on the outer edge of her own ear.

"Are you pulling my leg, Jannika?"

"Why yes, Leslie, I do believe I am," Jannika said.

They laughed as they continued to stroll down the brick sidewalk away from Market Square. Lee reached for Jannika's hand and gave it a little squeeze. Jannika squeezed back. Their footsteps slowed the closer they got to the parking lot.

"Are you parked here?" Jannika asked pointing to the lot.

"I'm the little green Toyota truck in the first row, right here."

They stopped on the sidewalk in front of Lee's truck.

"I had a wonderful night, Lee, great pizza, great conversation…" Jannika looked at the Maine plates on the green truck. "This might sound weird, but were you driving through Grangeton about a week ago?"

"I've been to Grangeton a couple of times in the past week or so, why?"

"I was on a not very great blind date and I saw a green pickup with Maine plates turn the corner onto Federal Street, and it reminded me of all the things I love about Maine and how I wished I was in Maine, or anywhere but on that date." Jannika worried she'd said too much and Lee would think she was some serial dater.

"That was you? If I had known, I would have pulled over and offered you a slice of pizza and—"

"And?"

Lee stepped in front of Jannika, reached for one of her hands, and smiled.

"I would have watched you eat it," Lee said as she moved closer to Jannika.

Lee was inches away from her. After all these years, she was here. Right here in front of her. Waiting for her, Jannika thought. Her heart was in her throat and she moved toward Lee. Her lips met Lee's. Desire ran through her body like a river. Her hands went under Lee's jacket to the small of Lee's back and pulled her closer. A soft low moan escaped from Jannika's throat. The excitement she held onto flooded through her body and her breath quickened.

Lee's lips responded to Jannika and answered with a hunger all their own. Lee wrapped her arms around Jannika, and her hands traveled down Jannika's spine. Lee kissed Jannika on her cheek, and then her lips moved down to her neck.

"Jannika Peterson, that was some kiss," Lee said, looking into Jannika's eyes.

"Whoa..." Jannika's breathing was heavy. She disengaged herself from Lee's embrace and took a wobbly step backward. Her left ankle twisted on the uneven bricks. "Yowcha!"

Lee reached out to steady her. "Are you okay?"

"Damn, damn, damnation. I twisted my ankle," Jannika said. She was trying to balance on one foot, with only the toe of her other foot touching the bricks. Any desire she'd felt left her body and was replaced by a shooting pain running up her leg.

"Let's sit in my truck and talk. It's getting pretty chilly out, and you should probably get off that ankle. Can you make it? Let me at least open the door for you," Lee said, moving around Jannika and opening the truck door.

"I can do it," said Jannika. She struggled with the best way to get into the truck, then grabbed the oh-shit handle and hauled herself up and into the truck.

"Funny, I don't remember you having a stubborn streak," Lee replied, smiling. "How's your ankle? Do you want me to have a look? I've had some First Aid training."

"No, thanks. It's not that bad. And to be honest, Lee, if you touch me I don't know what might happen." Jannika tried to smile.

"I'll go around to my side of the truck then." She hopped into the driver's seat but kept herself close to the door. "Jannika, you look so beautiful," Lee said. "Your eyes are reflecting your shirt or your shirt is reflecting your eyes—I can't tell, but it's incredible." She ran her hand through her hair and blew out a breath.

"I promised myself I wouldn't let myself get carried away by physical attraction, and here I am doing it again. And we both know I'm attracted to you." Jannika's words came out rushed. Maybe the sheer number of words would make a barrier between them.

Lee didn't move, but she looked at Jannika with such open wanting that Jannika felt lightheaded. "And I'm—"

Jannika interrupted Lee. "I'm confused between what was the past—you know, my silly crush on you—and what is happening now." She tried to look everywhere but Lee's face. "I don't want to make a fool of myself. Doesn't it feel strange to you?"

"Jannika, that was eighteen years ago. You were seventeen and I was twenty-four, right out of college. We were babies. I was flattered then that you had a crush on me..."

"I must have seemed so foolish." Jannika looked at Lee.

"You were adorable then, and you are even more adorable now. I took my responsibility to all the girls very seriously. I'm pretty sure you remember how seriously. But I'm forty-three now and you must be…"

"Thirty-five. I'm thirty-five," Jannika said. "Leslie…Lee." Jannika looked into Lee's eyes. "You're the first woman since my breakup with my ex a year ago that I've had any sort of attraction to or even desire to get to know better. When I was seventeen and felt like the world was against me, and my mother hated me, you listened. You listened to me for hours that summer. And I took your advice, you know. I never got the chance to tell you. You told me to start a journal and to write about all the things that were bothering me, but you also told me to write about all the things that were good. Even the tiny things, like the apple tree out back was all in blossoms today. I wrote about anything that made me feel good, even a little bit." Jannika looked out the windshield. "Thank you. If nothing else comes of our meeting again, I have the chance to say thank you to someone who helped me get through the last two years of living with my mother. I kept your words in my head. They gave me the courage to make a plan and leave my mother's house. Thank you, Lee." She reached over and touched Lee's hand.

Lee turned her hand over and their fingers wound together naturally. Jannika knew her hand was probably clammy and sticky, but she didn't pull it away. Lee's hand was warm and soft and dry. She looked back at Lee.

"How did that work out?" Lee asked.

"I worked while I was in community college and saved enough to leave."

Lee gave Jannika's hand a gentle squeeze. "And your relationship with your ex…? That sounds like it didn't end well."

"We met at a concert about five years ago. Instant attraction, fireworks, the whole thing. We flirted and left before the concert ended. Fast-forward a few weeks, and we decided to live together."

"In Portland? Or were you back in Stillmeadow?" Lee asked.

"No, I was living and working in Westbrook then, so it wasn't much of a commute to work. Joanne didn't want to give up her apartment in Portland. I thought we'd build a future together. I thought we were in love. I'm a romantic—too many books or something." She looked down at her hand, then slowly untangled it from Lee's.

"How long were you together?" Lee asked.

"Almost three years. She could be a bit jealous, but that was because her ex cheated on her several times. She had a hard time trusting people. And I could understand that, because I have my own stuff around trusting people with my father abandoning me and my mother when I was little." Jannika turned and leaned against the inside of the truck door, so she could look at Lee.

As she started to tell this story to Lee, she realized that blaming her breakup with Joanne for the way she protected her heart wasn't the truth. When she said the words *my father abandoning me* out loud in the small space of this truck cab, her words echoed back to her heart, and she knew it took many years to build all those layers of protection. All those years without her father, knowing he didn't care enough to stay around and didn't care enough to ever try to get in touch with her.

"What happened?" Lee asked gently.

She looked into Lee's welcoming eyes. The safety of her gaze enabled Jannika to continue.

"The short story is, Joanne's ex came back to visit some relatives. She'd moved out west someplace right after she and Joanne broke up. About a week later, I came home from work early on a Friday. I was going to surprise Joanne with her favorite supper. I pulled into the driveway, and there was a car I didn't recognize behind Joanne's truck."

"Oh no."

"Oh yes." Jannika looked down at her hands. "I didn't suspect anything. I figured one of her friends from work was over or something. When I got into the house I heard the shower running, which I thought was weird. I didn't see anyone else in the house. I knocked on the bathroom door and called to her, and two voices started swearing in response. I opened the door." She laughed nervously. "And the funny thing is that I still didn't suspect anything. In that instant, I thought that maybe they had gone for a hike and someone got hurt. I don't know what I was thinking, but it wasn't that my girlfriend was screwing around on me. But she was. With her ex. I backed the car out of the driveway and took off. When I came back, I expected Joanne to apologize or explain. Instead she screamed at me to get out and accused me of spying on her. She gave me until the end of the weekend to move out. After that she wouldn't answer my texts or emails or calls. Part of me wanted to stay there and see what would happen, but I was devastated. I just left. Like a dog with its tail between its legs."

"That's awful."

"For the next month or so, I tried to call her, text her, I wrote her letters. She wouldn't respond. It was like I never existed in her life." Jannika looked out at the parking lot. This was maybe the worst date conversation, worse than a med list. But it felt so good to tell someone.

"Did you two ever get a chance to talk about what happened that night?" Lee asked, reaching her hand toward Jannika. Jannika shifted away from Lee, and Lee mirrored her action and sat back against the seat.

"No, I haven't talked to her or seen her since the day she screamed at me." Jannika wiped the corner of her eye.

"I've got tissues, right here in the glove box," Lee said reaching over to unlatch it.

"No, I'm okay. Thanks," Jannika said. "I haven't talked to anyone about this except my friend Marcy."

Lee looked up at Jannika and brushed her fingertips down Jannika's cheek. Jannika had a powerful urge to lay her head on Lee's shoulder and let this gentle woman hold her. She couldn't remember the last time she was held and comforted.

"I'm so sorry, Jannika," Lee said.

Jannika reached up and took Lee's hand from her face, holding it for a moment before letting go. Lee shifted back to her side of the cab and put her hands in her lap. Jannika took a deep breath and let it out.

"Most of our friends started out as Joanne's friends, and you know how that goes, so I was thrilled when my Aunt Gunnie called me to tell me about the job at The Pageturner. I came down, applied, got the job, made some great friends, and am determined to build a new life down here."

"That sounds like a perfect plan." Lee thought for a few moments before speaking more. She didn't want to scare Jannika away by telling her how powerful her attraction was. She'd watched at lunch and at dinner how Jannika would move toward her and flirt and joke for a few minutes, and then catch herself and withdraw. But she could be patient. She didn't mind working for what she wanted, and she wasn't afraid of obstacles. There was something about Jannika that made her feel like she would slay dragons, climb mountains, swim oceans, just to be near her. She turned to face Jannika and put her arm on the back of the seat.

"Thanks for telling me about your ex. It didn't look easy for you to tell me. I want you to know how much I appreciate your honesty. I meant it when I said that I wanted to get to know you, and I do. Can we take it day by day?"

Jannika ran her fingers through her thick short blond hair.

"For the record, you are adorable when you do that," Lee said, smiling. The urge to kiss Jannika was so strong. Lee swore her lips were still tingling from their earlier kiss.

"And you have the most incredible smile. Thanks for listening."

"I want to stay true to my word about taking things day by day," Lee said, "but if I don't get you back to your car right now, I'm afraid I may have to kiss you, like you kissed me a little while ago." Lee moved her hand from the back of the seat to the side of Jannika's face and traced a line from Jannika's temple to her jawline and over to her chin. She looked into Jannika's eyes. "Unless you want me to kiss you." Lee's voice was soft. She felt warmth move through her body.

"Oh, Lee." Jannika leaned forward, her breath quick.

Lee could see the conflict on Jannika's face. She didn't want to come on too fast and too strong, but the effect of Jannika sitting just inches away was overriding her good intentions. Her body was reacting in a way it hadn't since before she lost her wife. All she could think about was that kiss. She leaned back into the driver's seat and tapped the dash with her right hand.

"Okay. Where is your car parked?" she asked.

"It's up two streets on your right, there's a little parking lot up there. And...thanks." The truck cab was silent for the short ride.

Lee pulled the truck next to Jannika's car and immediately got out. She didn't know if she could resist Jannika and that beautiful face, that gorgeous mouth, again tonight. She opened Jannika's door.

"How's the ankle?" Lee asked.

"Not as bad as I thought it would be." Jannika waved Lee's outstretched hand away. "I'm okay. Thanks for...in the truck... taking things day to day sounds good." She limped to her car. "I had a great time tonight, except for the ankle bit."

"I had a wonderful night too. Except for, you know." Lee smiled and pointed to Jannika's ankle. She was happy that her decision to pull back from kissing Jannika again was the right one. "Can you drive okay?"

"Yup, thanks, have a good night," Jannika said.

"Bye then." She waved as Jannika's car pulled out. Lee got back into her truck and sighed.

"Quite a night, Lee, quite a night." She leaned back against the seat, closing her eyes. She smiled. Jannika Peterson was a complicated woman. And Lee was ready for a challenge. She thought about Jannika's profile in the nighttime shadows of the truck cab. Jannika had a sexy haircut, short in the back and longer in the front. It accentuated her smooth jawline and the elegant curve of her neck. Lee thought about putting her lips on that neck and feeling her hot breath come back at her as her lips traveled down that curve. A low groan escaped her throat, and she shifted in her seat and gripped the steering wheel.

"Oh my." She turned the key in the ignition. She needed to get home.

Chapter Eleven

Jannika hit the snooze on her alarm again and rolled over onto her back, gingerly opening her tired and puffy eyes. She'd tossed and turned all night, thinking about the date with Lee. Her face grew warm as she thought about the dream that woke her in the middle of the night. She stretched her body and ran her hand down her stomach and onto her thigh. But she didn't have to dream about Lee—they'd kissed the night before. Oh, that kiss. Her lips seemed to have a direct line to other areas of her body. She didn't know a kiss could feel like that. She replayed last night's sidewalk scene in her mind several times.

She glanced over at the clock. "Holy crap, it's late." She threw on some clothes, ran a brush through her hair and another over her teeth, grabbed her jacket, keys, and tote bag, and was out the door and at the bookstore in twenty minutes. Her ankle was still sore, but she could walk on it.

"Delivery for Miss Jannika." Andy from the Polish bakery came into the store, holding a bakery box tied with string.

"Oh, Andy, thank you," Jannika said, taking the box and placing it on her desk.

"I'm supposed to tell you there's a card inside. See ya, Jannika." Andy turned and left the store.

Jannika untied the box and peeked inside. A half dozen oatmeal raisin cookies, still warm from the oven, lay waiting for her. She picked up the card. *Jannika, thank you for a wonderful evening. I hope your ankle is feeling better. Lee.* Jannika smiled. She felt cared for and special. She pulled a cookie out from the box. She didn't want to miss the still-warmness, the perfection of the first bite, when the cookie would bend, then fall into her mouth. She was happy there weren't any customers yet. She didn't want anything to interfere with that first bite of warm cookie. The phone rang. She let it ring a few times so she could take another bite.

"The Pageturner, this is Jannika," she said and hoped the caller couldn't hear her chewing.

"Hi, Jannika, it's Lee. Sorry to call you at work. We didn't exchange phone numbers last night. I think we both may have been distracted. I wanted to tell you...I had a wonderful time last night."

"Oh, Lee, thank you. And thanks for the cookies. Oatmeal raisin is my favorite, and they brought them over still warm from the oven. Mm, I had one and it was perfect."

"Could you say that again?" Lee asked.

"What?"

"You said oatmeal raisin is your favorite and they were still warm. But it was what you said after that."

"What? Mm?" Jannika liked teasing and flirting with Lee. It was like she was able to put down a weight she didn't know she was carrying. She felt lighter. She felt happy. She wanted to get a response from Lee.

"Oh my, yes," Lee said, her voice dropping. Jannika felt her heart quicken.

"Apologies. I know you're at work, and this isn't the time for..."

"For...?" Jannika wished she wasn't at work. She wanted to flirt with Lee in person.

"For playful banter," Lee said. Jannika could hear Lee grinning on the other end of the phone. "I was wondering, if your ankle is up to it, would you like to go apple picking this weekend? I saw a sign for an apple orchard on the road to my house, something-something meadows? Do you even like apples?" Lee laughed.

"My ankle is much better, not swollen at all. I have to admit my mind wasn't on where I was walking last night. And yes, I like apples, and yes, I would love to go apple picking this weekend. I work on Saturday, but I'm free on Sunday."

"That works for me. What time on Sunday, and what was your mind on?"

"How about I meet you at Green Meadow Orchard at ten o'clock? I think they'll still have some cider doughnuts left. They pretty much make them all day during picking season." Jannika walked with the phone to the end of the store aisles and glanced around to make sure customers hadn't slipped into the store while she wasn't paying attention. "My mind was on a very beautiful woman and her lips."

"I'll make a note to buy you cookies more often. They seem to have an interesting effect on you."

They exchanged phone numbers and email addresses and it took them about three tries to say good-bye. Neither of them wanted to be the first to hang up. This was silly, thought Jannika, as she turned around and put the bookstore phone on the long counter behind her. She smiled. And kind of wonderful. She was glad that Lee had suggested a daytime date. Lee had heard her when she told her she wanted to take this one step at a time. She listened and she respected Jannika's wishes. The next few days would drag by.

❖

At closing on Saturday, Jannika shut off the last of the lights and said, "Good night, little bookstore," as she locked the door. She stopped at Joy Wok and picked up some pork fried rice and sweet and sour chicken on her way home. She didn't want to cook tonight. She planned on a Saturday spa night before the apple picking date tomorrow. She used to do spa nights a long time ago, before she met Joanne, but Joanne thought spa nights at home were silly when you could make an appointment and go to a spa.

She finished the last of her plate and put the leftovers in the fridge. She went in the bathroom to check on her tub—almost full. She took off her gray corduroys, peeled off her socks, unbuttoned her soft blue shirt, and unhooked her bra. Oops, she'd forgotten her special spa music. She grabbed her robe off the hook on the back of the bathroom door and padded out to the living room. She searched the shelf of old CDs above her sound system, pulling a *Wondrous Wind Chimes* CD from the shelf and putting it on repeat. She flipped a second wall switch in the bathroom and the sound of ocean waves and tinkling wind chimes filled the room. Jannika loved this cottage and the care that her landlords had taken when they remodeled it. Each room was wired for sound.

"Perfect. Perfecto. Perfection." She smiled as she hung her robe back on the hook, then took off her underwear and flipped it into the hamper. Jannika stepped into the tub and lowered herself into the warm water, unfolding her legs as she sat down. She leaned back against the tub and let the steam work its magic on her skin. She hadn't heard from Lee since their phone call. Was Lee waiting for her to call or text her? She rubbed honey almond soap into the bath sponge and ran the sponge up and down her wet arms.

She didn't want to give Lee mixed signals. A phone call might make it seem like she wanted things to move faster, and she didn't. Well...part of her did, and part of her didn't. She wasn't sure what the right thing was to do. She soaped the sponge again and rubbed it on her belly. A picture of Lee flashed in her mind and stayed. Lee looking at her after they kissed. Lee looking into her, seeing her, embracing all of Jannika. Lee's face flushed, her eyes full of desire. The ripples of water caressed Jannika's skin, and they were Lee. Lee's fingers, Lee's hands. Jannika's thighs trembled and her back tightened and arched. If only her mind could be as sure as her body was.

❖

Jannika pulled her car into Green Meadow Orchard's parking lot at nine fifty-five a.m. Her excitement coupled with a caffeine buzz had her fingerless-gloved hands tapping the steering wheel. She scanned the parking lot for Lee's truck and didn't see it. Her mind began a round of anxiety questions. Should she get out and wander around over by the pumpkins? Or should she get out and sit on one of the bales of hay by the parking lot fence? No, that would look posed, she'd look like someone trying a bit too hard. "I guess I'll sit here and wait," she mumbled to herself.

She watched as several couples with children pulled up and got out of their vans and SUVs. Jannika liked the idea of children but could never make up her mind if she wanted her own. She couldn't get past the thought of the possibility of hurting a child the way her father had hurt her. Her head whipped to her left at the sound of gravel crunching next to her car.

"Good morning," Lee called as she waved gloved hands at Jannika's car window.

Jannika grabbed her black skinny down jacket, got out of her car, and slipped the jacket on. "Good morning to you too." Her voice was an octave too high, probably another effect of the half a pot of tea she drank before she got to the orchard. Lee raised her eyebrows, probably wondering why she sounded like she'd huffed helium, but her smile didn't change.

"Have you been here before?" Lee asked. They both turned toward the gravel walkway next to the large red barn.

"I come by to grab a pie or some cider, but I haven't been apple picking since I lived in Maine," Jannika replied. She ran her gloved hand along the fence rail and hopped her hand over each fence post as they walked up to the barn.

"Are you picking?" asked the young woman who sat inside a little white shingled box with a roof that looked a lot like a wishing well. At their nods, she handed them each a small white paper bag with a big apple stamped in red on the front and back.

"Where do we go?" Jannika asked. The young woman gave Jannika a big wide smile, her eyes lingering on Jannika's face for a couple of seconds before she replied. She hoped Lee didn't notice.

"Follow the red arrows down this lane and someone will show you where to pick. What variety are you lookin' for?" The young woman focused her attention entirely on her, completely ignoring Lee.

"I'm going to make a pie later, so I'm looking for Cortlands," Jannika said, her words coming out in a rush. She was never comfortable with other women flirting or admiring her. She never knew how to respond or if she should respond. She was on a date with Lee, not apple woman.

"And I want some Honeycrisps," Lee said.

"I bet you make a great pie." The young woman tipped her head to the side a bit and looked up at Jannika and then leaned forward and looked at Jannika's hands. "Yes, I bet you do." She took a deep breath. "Okay, then. Both of those are down the path and up a small hill on your right. There'll be signs."

"Great, thanks. We'll return," said Lee brightly, and she set off down the grass lane, swinging her paper bag.

Jannika's boots moved through the wet grass and in a few steps she caught up with Lee.

"Did you catch Miss Red Flannel in the booth giving you the eye?" Lee turned and looked at Jannika.

"Oh, really? I didn't notice anything," Jannika said. She didn't turn to look at Lee and tried not to smile.

"I have to make a confession, and you should probably know this about me." Lee stopped.

Jannika stopped walking too and held her paper bag with both hands. She felt the armor near her tender heart draw in close. She looked at Lee.

"Here goes," Lee said.

Was Lee blushing? A small stripe of pink showed on her cheekbones and neck, not fiery red like one of Jannika's blushes. She had never seen Lee blush before.

"I like it when other women admire the woman I am with. I feel proud and happy to be with such a beautiful woman and love when other women acknowledge that too. In fact"—Lee leaned toward a stunned Jannika—"it makes me a little hot and bothered, if you know what I mean." Lee waggled her eyebrows up and down. "Too much information?" Lee tipped her head to the side with the unanswered question.

Jannika tried to get her jaw to work so she could speak. It had come a bit unhinged. Nothing and no one had prepared her for this woman. She shook her head. "No, that's fine. I mean, that's great, I guess...Okay, I'm not sure what I mean. You mean you aren't jealous?"

"Jealous? Gosh, there's nothing to be jealous of. I'm not a jealous person. I'm more a grateful person, a person who appreciates things, appreciates life." Lee's face grew solemn and her eyes went a bit flat and expressionless. "I know how fast life can change."

"Your wife, I'm sorry I forgot her—"

"Shannon, that's her name. Sometimes five years seems forever and sometimes it feels like yesterday," Lee said.

"You haven't told me much about Shannon or your life with her. I hope someday when the time seems right, you will. I want to know about you." She stepped a little closer to Lee and looked into her eyes. "I want to know everything."

Jannika continued to look into Lee's eyes as families and couples on their way up the path walked around them. She barely noticed them. All she saw were Lee's eyes looking into hers asking a question. She replied with a look and a smile. Lee reached over and took Jannika's hand.

"Jannika," she said, her voice soft and low. "Let's get some apples and then let's go over to my house."

"Okay," Jannika whispered.

They climbed the short hill to the area marked for picking, their shoulders bumping every now and then. Jannika picked her bag of Cortlands for apple pie and Lee picked her bag of Honeycrisps. Lee took an apple out of her bag as they headed back down the hill.

"That was the fastest apple picking expedition I've ever been on," she said with a laugh. "Hungry?" Lee handed Jannika the apple.

"Me too." Jannika returned the laugh and took the apple. She rubbed it on the front of her shirt, licked her bottom lip, and parted her lips around the red skin. She bit into the apple with slow precision. She looked at Lee as juice ran down her chin.

"Girl, what you do to me," Lee said, shaking her head.

Jannika wiped her chin with the back of her hand. "I'm sorry," Jannika said with a mouthful of apple.

"You are so not sorry," Lee said.

"Right. I am so not sorry." Jannika laughed.

Jannika caught Lee watching her legs as they walked. She liked when Lee looked at her. She usually felt self-conscious when women noticed her body, but not with Lee. She felt beautiful. Lee held out her hand and she switched her apple bag to her left hand, took Lee's hand, and gave it a squeeze. They paid Miss Red Flannel for the apples and grabbed their bags from the pitted wood counter.

"How about you follow me to my place," Lee said.

"Sounds like a plan," Jannika said.

"It's up the road on the right," Lee pointed into the trees.

Jannika put her bag of apples on the floor of the back seat and wrapped the small blanket she always kept in the car around the bag. She hoped they wouldn't roll all over the place. She followed Lee as she took a left out of the parking lot and headed up the road. They had gone only about a half a mile when Jannika saw Lee's right taillight blinking.

Right up the road and she'd be with Lee. She took a deep breath. She wasn't exactly anxious, more excited and happy. *Go with it, Jannika.* Happy was good. She turned the car onto a dirt driveway, lined with golden sugar maples. Leaves dotted the stone walls on both sides of the driveway. The trees were so old they formed a golden canopy overhead. She felt like she was driving into a storybook.

The canopy opened to reveal a simple white farmhouse with a small ell. Across the driveway on the right were a small red barn and a couple of acres of hay fields. She pulled up behind Lee, parked, and jumped out of the car.

"Lee, this is gorgeous. How did you find it?"

"My friend Bill, one of the rangers I work with. His father owned this place, and he passed away last year. The place has been in the family for years, but none of them wants to live here. They don't want to give it up either, so they were looking for someone to live here and watch over things. I came and took a look and..." Lee held out her hands, palms up.

"There was no *and*, was there? I bet it was love at first sight." Jannika caught her double entendre as the words left her mouth and knew her face had turned a deep shade of red. She tried to change the subject as quickly as possible. "Would you show me around?"

"I'd love to," Lee said, taking her hand. "First, I'll show you the house, then the barn."

She followed Lee up the stairs to the ell and into the mudroom. The house had original wide pine board floors, and the kitchen had been updated but kept the farmhouse style with a soapstone sink and a big six-burner stove. It was an eat-in kitchen and a farmhouse table and chairs sat next to a big picture window that looked out to the fields.

"I'd sit down with a cup of tea and never leave," Jannika said.

"Sometimes I wish I could do just that. I love that view. I've seen deer, rabbits, turkeys, foxes, and an occasional heron. There must be a pond nearby, but I haven't found it yet. I can't wait to see the show this winter and next spring." Lee turned and smiled at Jannika.

"That would be Baker's Pond. My aunt used to bring me skating there when I was little. I'll show you sometime." She liked knowing Lee intended to be around for a while.

Lee brought her through the rest of the house. She tried to read the titles of the books on the bookshelves in the living room as they passed through. She loved the braided rug and woodstove and all the small wood sculptures of birds and animals that lined an antique cabinet. There was a tiny bathroom in what probably used to be a closet, and a huge screened porch outside the front door. Lee opened the screen door and held out her hand once again to clasp Jannika's.

"Now for the best part," Lee said leading her over a crooked flagstone walkway toward the barn. The flagstones stopped about halfway there.

"Why do the flagstones stop here and turn back toward the kitchen in the back of the house? I wonder why they didn't continue the path all the way to the barn," Jannika said.

"The stones go to where the well used to be. One path from the front of the house and one path from the back. Can you picture it?" Lee asked.

"I can."

Lee grabbed the big wooden barn door handle and slid the door to the side. Then she reached inside to the right and flipped a switch. The barn smelled like dirt and wood, old hay and a hint of animals—horse? cow? pig?—Jannika couldn't tell which. There was a large center aisle and a ladder that went up to the hayloft. Small wood pens were lined up on the left. Jannika thought they were probably for pigs. On the right, there was what looked like a huge horse stall. Lee stood with her hand on its door, then slid the door on its track to the right.

"Jannika. Come look."

She stepped up beside Lee and looked into the big stall. There was a huge workbench in the center, and smaller benches lined the three walls. Woodworking tools of all shapes and sizes hung on the walls. Several small piles of wood shavings were on the floor. Jannika walked close to the center workbench.

"Are these yours?" she asked.

"It's my hobby. It's what I do when I'm not at the park," Lee said, picking up a small hand-carved bird. The little chickadee sat in an intricate carving of a human hand, its palm slightly curved to hold the bird. She put the chickadee in Jannika's hand.

"Oh my God, Lee, these are beautiful." She looked at the other carvings on shelves around the room and the sketches tacked up on one of the barn beams near the door.

"I remember you always whittling little animals out of wood scraps at camp. So the animals I saw on the shelf in your living room...?"

"Yes, those are mine."

"I didn't know you were an artist. Do you sell them? How could you sell them?" she asked, still holding the little bird and rubbing her thumb along the wing. She thought about the care and skill it must take to carve these small creatures. Each one seemed filled with beauty and peace. She pictured Lee in this workshop, her hands taking such care to carve these birds and animals. She remembered her at camp, sitting on her cabin's steps, carving things. She looked at Lee's hands.

"Sometimes I go to craft fairs, and I have an Etsy shop online. I love sharing them with people who are drawn to them. And the cash helps out a lot in the winter," Lee said. She stepped closer to Jannika and put her hand under Jannika's hand. The hand holding the little wood bird. "You know, you're holding it exactly the way I carved the hand over there on the bench to hold it, with your thumb barely touching the wing. This one must belong to you," Lee said, looking into Jannika's eyes.

"Oh no, I couldn't, Lee," Jannika said, moving to place the little bird back in the wooden hand. When Lee's hand cradled hers, the hairs on her arm rose.

"You are adorable and slightly dangerous. You know that, don't you?"

"How am I dangerous?" Jannika asked.

"There is something a bit mysterious about you. Something beyond anyone's grasp. But it doesn't make you seem unreachable. It makes me curious, intrigued. It makes you incredibly desirable." Lee stepped forward, put her hands on Jannika's waist, and kissed her. Jannika felt the warmth of Lee's body radiating on hers as Lee's hands drew her closer.

"Did you just kiss me?" Jannika asked moving her hands up Lee's arms to rest around the back of her neck.

"Yes, I do believe I did," Lee said.

"Do it again," Jannika whispered, her lips inches from Lee's.

Lee's hands, hips, and mouth moved in one motion, drawing Jannika even closer. She kissed her long and deep, the pressure of her lips and gentleness of her tongue telling Jannika what the rest of her body wanted. Jannika's body sang, and her hands moved over Lee's shoulders and arms, then around to the small of her back, and inched down to the roundness below. Lee stepped back and took Jannika's hands in hers.

"Not here, Jannika," she said, her voice rumbling low with desire. "This way." Lee took Jannika's hand and led her back to the house. They stopped and kissed again when they got outside the barn. Then they kissed again when they reached the old well site. As they approached the ell of the farmhouse, Jannika grabbed Lee's hand and gave it a tug. Lee turned around and Jannika pushed up against her, kissing her and running her hands down the curve of Lee's hips. Lee's back was against the door.

"Yes." Lee's breath was jagged. She reached behind to open the door. They stepped into the ell, threw off their jackets, kicked off their shoes, and walked, kissed, and stumbled through the ell and the kitchen, giggling and laughing.

"Come get me." Lee bounded up the stairs.

"Right behind you and loving the view."

Jannika's phone rang in her back pocket. She pulled her phone out and looked at it.

"Damn, I have to take this." She answered the call. "Yes. How did it happen?"

Lee listened to the one-way conversation and watched Jannika pace back and forth in the small hallway outside her bedroom.

"Lee, I'm so sorry. That was one of my Aunt Gunnie's friends. She said my aunt is okay but she's at the emergency room. She collapsed when they were playing cribbage and they're doing some tests." She shook her head. "I have to leave. I'm so sorry."

"Absolutely, do you want me to go with you?"

Jannika was already halfway down the stairs.

"No, that's okay. I'll text you after I get there and let you know how she is."

Jannika ran to the ell. Lee found her there lacing up her boots. Jannika looked up, and Lee saw a question there, but she didn't know what to say.

"She has to be okay." Jannika grabbed her jacket. "I've got to go."

Lee thought she saw tears brimming in Jannika's eyes when she opened the door. "Let me know," Lee said.

"I will." Jannika jogged to her car.

Lee watched Jannika start her car and fly down the driveway. Stones and road dust flew out behind the spinning tires as the car disappeared.

Chapter Twelve

O h no," Lee said with her jaw set. Anytime she witnessed someone driving dangerously, it brought back Shannon's accident. She'd feel it in her gut first, then her heart, before her mind could even respond. She took a few deep breaths and let them out slowly. Her days were mostly okay now. But sometimes at night the hollow ache of loss would keep her awake. Anytime she saw reckless driving, the shock and panic she'd felt when she heard about Shannon's accident was front and center.

The pine boards creaked as she paced in her kitchen. She picked up her phone. She put it down again. She wanted to call Jannika and make sure she got to the hospital okay. She sat at the big pine trestle table in the farmhouse kitchen with the phone in her hand. Her stomach hurt with worry.

She put the phone in her pocket and went out to the ell. She came back with an armload of wood. On her fourth trip her phone chimed. She needed to be physically active when she was upset. She wasn't someone who let life happen to her—she constructed her life, as much as she could. She'd learned as the oldest of six kids to make do with some things, and her artistic gift gave her the creativity to problem solve in unexpected ways. Her family joked and called her MacGyver. She saw life and its challenges as an opportunity to grow, not a burden to be tolerated.

She threw a couple of pieces of wood on the woodstove, put on the pot of pumpkin soup she had made for their lunch, and turned down the draft. She liked that the house came with a Jøtul woodstove that had a cookplate built into the top. It reminded her of home, and it was efficient to use the heat already produced by the woodstove. While the soup was getting hot, she went out to the woodshed to replace wood in the ell. The sun was wine red and low in the sky at the edge of the field, and the temperature was dropping fast.

"Four trips with the wheelbarrow should do it." Her breath made small clouds when she spoke. Talking to herself was a habit she'd picked up as a park manager while often working alone in the woods. When she was younger, it had helped her feel less alone. Talking out loud also helped her work out problems. Over the years the habit had become second nature, though she often startled the new part-time park staff when they came upon her in the woods. She laughed at that memory as she steered the wheelbarrow on its last trip to the ell, unloaded the wood, and checked on the soup again. It was hot and she could smell the maple syrup she'd added.

As she ate the soup, she texted her sister Bonnie. *Hey Bon-Bon, I finished loading wood and thought of you. What's up in your world?*

Bonnie replied, *The kids have some friends over for an overnight. Yes, I'm crazy. They're playing a popcorn game in the playroom downstairs. They say it's a game, but I think it's just an excuse to throw popcorn around.* The kids' antics were always a good distraction when Lee was stressed.

Met a woman. Like her. A lot.

WHOA... this wasn't just another one-time date?

One lunch, one pizza dinner, and we went apple picking today.

And...?

She had to leave, family emergency.

Let me get Mike to take over kid duty and call you.
    K

A few minutes later, she filled Bonnie in on the past week and the way Jannika left that afternoon. When she got to the part about Jannika peeling out of the driveway, she felt her back stiffen.

"You're pissed at her for ripping out of your driveway," Bonnie said.

She couldn't deny it. "You know I can't deal with that. If that's the way she handles a car when she's upset..."

"I know, I know. Have you talked to her about Shannon?" Bonnie asked.

"Yes."

"About how she died?"

"I told her it was a car accident, but not the details."

"You said, you think she cares about you too, right? That you can feel that, right? Then you need to sit down and talk with her. Tell her the whole story. It's not like you to put up a wall and walk away from someone you think you care about. I've got that right, right? You think this could be serious with her?"

"I think it might already be, and that's causing a bit of flutter around my heart, you know? I trust it. I trust my heart, but when she flew off in the car like that, it caught me for a minute," Lee said.

"And then you stacked five cords of wood, right?"

"Not quite." Lee laughed. "And then I missed all of you. I'm at my new park and we're off from November till March, so I'll be able to come up for the holidays and have some nice long visits."

"Why don't you come up next weekend? The kids would love to see you, and I'll get Mom and Dad to come over too. We'll have a big meal, and we'll cure you of your homesickness for a while, right?" Bonnie said.

"I'm sure it will."

"Come up. We miss you."

"Okay, I'll come on Saturday. Thanks for being there, Bon."

"Here's a phone hug."

"And one for you. Love you." She put her phone in her back pocket and went upstairs to change into some more comfortable clothes. She still felt a little edgy from this afternoon and figured she would work on the sign designs for her park.

Most times the division hired out to have the signs routed and ready for the spring, but she'd offered to make up the new signs needed this year. Sign making was different from carving. She had experimented a couple of weeks ago and needed to tweak the designs a bit. She headed to her shop, the perfect distraction. She needed something to focus on besides Jannika's laugh, after she bit that apple, and her crazy-long legs that, in Lee's mind, kept wrapping themselves around Lee's waist. And she was angry at Jannika for racing her car down the driveway. Jannika obviously didn't know how quickly things could change your life forever.

Lee looked over at the place where Jannika stood when they'd kissed, just a few hours ago. The jig slipped. "Oh, damn!" She turned off the equipment and leaned against the workbench. The barn was not the right place for her now.

❖

Jannika had a heavy foot on the gas the entire way to the hospital on the other side of Grangeton. She flew through a yellow light that blinked to red on River Road a half mile before the Grangeton Hospital. *She has to be all right.* She repeated that mantra until she entered the emergency room.

"Gunilla Anderson. My aunt. She was brought here by ambulance?"

"Come with me." A woman in scrubs led her down a short hallway and pulled open the curtains surrounding the bed, closing them again after her.

"Auntie, what happened?" Jannika held out her hand to a woman standing by her aunt's bed. "Hi, I'm Jannika. Thank you for everything."

The woman returned the handshake. "I'm Carol, Gunnie's friend. She's okay."

"I'm in the room. I can speak for myself." Gunnie's voice often surprised people. No one expected such a robust voice to come from such a diminutive woman. "I'm fine. It was my sugar. This is a whole lot of fuss about nothing."

"They're doing some tests," Carol said quietly.

"I can still hear, ladies." Gunnie pulled the sheet up to her chest and tucked it under her arms.

"What happened?" Jannika pulled up a plastic chair and took her aunt's hand in hers.

"I felt a little peaked, then the next thing I knew I was riding in the back of an ambulance. Whole lot of bother for nothing. I just needed my snack. Carol wouldn't let me go until you got here." She sat up. "I'm ready."

"Auntie, I just got here. Let's wait until your tests come back, okay? Carol, what happened?"

"We were playing cribbage when her hands started to shake, and then she got all pale. I asked her if she needed some food, because I know all about her sugar, but she sort of folded up and slid off her chair on the floor. I think she fainted. I called 9-1-1 and put a cold cloth on her head. She was starting to wake up, but I told her not to move until the EMTs came. She got all perky after they put an IV in her."

"I'm so glad you were with her." She squeezed her aunt's hand and smiled up at Carol.

"Carol," Gunnie said, "you can go on home. I know you have to start fixing dinner for Harlow."

"Are you sure? I can go outside and call him." Carol fiddled with her wedding ring.

"No, no, no. Nick is here, and I'm fine. I'll call you later."

"Okay then, if you're sure."

"Carol..."

Carol gave Gunnie's other hand a squeeze and had a little trouble finding the opening in the cloth curtains surrounding the bed but, after a few wild gropes, made her way out.

Gunnie Anderson did not look seventy, even today, sitting in a hospital bed in a faded johnny, her makeup all but worn off, and her hair mussed. Her one extravagance was to visit her friend Carol's Cut Hut to keep her favorite haircut and color. The severe cut of her hair and her sharp nose and jawline gave her a formidable look. Gunnie cultivated that impression out of habit. She was the outlier in her family. Everyone else was over five eight, but she stood at five three. Gunnie always told it like it was, while the rest of the family was deafeningly silent when it came to honest emotions. Jannika loved her more than anyone.

"Nick, take me home. I don't like hospitals."

Jannika's phone rang. "Sorry, Auntie." She looked at the phone and silenced it. "Shit." Great, just who she wanted to hear from today. What was next, locusts?

"Jannika Elana Peterson." Gunnie shook her head.

"Sorry."

"Who is it? Something wrong at the store?"

"It was Joanne's number."

"Joanne from up north? That tramp, what does she want, calling you after all this time. Don't call her back. You're down here now, you have your store. And you're dating, I heard?"

"I'll check my messages later. Who told you I went out on a date?" Jannika wanted to check to see if Joanne left a message. But her aunt needed her and she tried to focus on her.

"Carol told me. Leonard from the hardware store was over at Portsmouth and told Laura he saw you with a woman in a parking lot. He was going to go over to see if you were okay. But as he got closer he could see you were in good hands. So to speak." Gunnie chuckled. "Laura babysits for Carol's grandkids sometimes."

"Of course, so if Carol your hairdresser knows, all of Grangeton knows."

"Probably all of Fairfield too." Gunnie put her hand over her mouth to muffle her laughter.

Jannika laughed too. She had a love/hate relationship with small town life. She loved that there were people like Leonard looking out for her, but she hated the gossip. She was surprised that by the time the story got to her aunt it was still reasonably accurate.

The curtains parted, and a young woman in scrubs held a clipboard out to Aunt Gunnie.

"Everything came back fine, Mrs. Anderson. Someone will be in to remove your IV, and then you're a free woman. Just sign this. There are instructions for you to see your regular doctor as soon as possible to try to regulate your blood sugar a bit better. You aren't diabetic, but you might be a bit hypoglycemic. You need to follow up with your doctor. Okay?"

"I will." Gunnie waved her hand at her and took the pen.

A young man came in and removed the IV from Gunnie's arm. Jannika wanted to help her get dressed, but Gunnie would have none of that.

"I'm not an invalid. Close these curtains and I'll be ready in a jiff."

"I'll take your pocketbook and wait right here for you." Jannika looped Gunnie's pocketbook over her shoulder and closed the curtains behind her.

"She's a feisty one," the clipboard woman said as she fast-walked past Jannika.

You don't know the half of it. Jannika thanked the universe for that every day.

While she waited, she couldn't resist the compulsion to check her phone. Joanne had left voicemail. She used her voice-to-text app and read it. Joanne was selling the house and had found some of her stuff.

"I'm ready. How do I get out of here?" Gunnie's hands beat at the curtains.

Jannika found the opening and pulled the curtain to the side. "Here I am, Auntie. I'll carry your pocketbook, and why don't you hold on to my arm."

"I'll do no such thing." She took Jannika's hand as they left the ER. "I know you were worried, but I'm fine, just fine. The experts said so. Now please give that bag over to me and take me home. You can tell me all about your date."

Jannika drove her aunt home and filled her in on her dates with Lee. She got her settled at the kitchen table and put some leftover pot roast and carrots to warm up in the oven. Aunt Gunnie didn't trust microwaves and refused to own one.

"She sounds like a great girl. But you don't sound convinced of that."

"I like her. I'm just being cautious."

"Don't be too cautious. You need to live your life, not just think about living it. Now tell me about the other one. What did she want after all this time?"

"Joanne is selling the house. That's why she sent me a message. She found some of my stuff and wants me to come up and get it." Jannika opened the cabinet and took down a plate and water glass for her aunt.

"What *stuff*? If it was anything you needed, you would have missed it by now. You don't need to see her again." Jannika put cutlery around the plate. "I can do that, you know."

"I know, but let me fuss over you tonight. You've had an unusual day. Believe me, part of me just wants to ignore the whole thing, but I never got to tell Joanne that it's over. My gut is telling me I need to do that. I'll be okay, Auntie."

"She's a tramp and when you caught her...you know what... she threw you out of your house."

"Technically it was her house." She kissed Gunnie's cheek. "Let's not talk about it today. You need to have some food and rest."

"Nick, don't go up there. You like it here. You have the store, and you love your cottage." Gunnie looked up at her from her seat at the table. "Oh, by the way, about the store. Now this is probably nothing, but Carol told me she heard that Joe was talking about the bother of the store. You know Carol, I'm sure she's heard it on the fifth or sixth pass around."

Jannika looked at her aunt and saw the love and longing in her face. She realized that it wasn't just that her aunt didn't want her to get hurt again, but how much she loved having Jannika close by. She sat at the table next to Gunnie and took one of her hands.

"Joe Bosworth said something to that effect to me the last time I talked to him, and it does make me worry, now that I know his history with businesses. I do love the store and my cottage, but what I love most of all is being close to you. I love that you drop by the store and invite me over for dinner. I love that I can drive over to talk to you in person instead of on the phone. I don't want to lose that." She wasn't sure who she was trying to reassure, herself or her aunt.

Gunnie squeezed Jannika's hand. "I can get the roast out of the oven myself. Why don't you go home and call your date— Lee, is it? Go have your supper with her."

Jannika kissed her again and got up from the table. "Are you sure you'll be okay?"

"I'm sure. If you want me to rest, you need to go, because we'll keep on jawin'."

"Call me if you need anything. And I mean anything, okay?" She knew her aunt was right and she didn't want to tire her out. But she was a little worried still.

"I need you to call that girl. Promise me."

Jannika went to the oven and opened the door to check on the food. "Promise. Your supper should be ready in another ten or fifteen minutes or so."

"I know how to cook. I'll call you in the morning."

"Okay, Auntie." Jannika bent and kissed her good-bye and headed to her car.

Jannika got in her car and checked her phone before starting the engine. There was a text from Joanne.

Did you get my message? Answer me.

She didn't want to worry Gunnie by sitting in the driveway texting. She knew her aunt would be looking out the window to wave good-bye. She started the car, and sure enough, there was her aunt, in the window. Jannika waved back as she backed out of the driveway and onto the street.

During the three-mile drive home, her mind spun between the text from Joanne, her Aunt Gunnie's health, Joe Bosworth and the store, and Lee. She brought the apples from the farm into the cottage and put the bag in the fridge. She made a cup of tea and sat on the couch and looked out the sliding doors at the end of her small living room.

Jannika brought her feet up onto the couch and stuffed an orange pillow behind her back. She stayed there curled up, watching the afternoon sun sink behind the pine trees in the back yard.

Her phone chirped again. It was Lee. *How is your aunt?*

She replied, *Sorry, I just got home. My aunt is ok. Low blood sugar. She's home now.*

I bet you haven't eaten. Would you like company? I have some tasty soup I could bring over?

Jannika thought for a half minute, then tapped Lee's number. She'd promised her aunt, after all.

"Hey there," Lee answered.

"This might sound silly, but I wanted to hear your voice," Jannika said.

"That doesn't sound silly to me at all. I'm so glad your aunt is okay. It sounds like you're really close to her."

"Probably closer than to my mother. She's always been my anchor, so tough, and today she looked so vulnerable in that hospital bed. It shook me a little. Sorry I left like that." Jannika heard only silence on the phone. "Lee, are you still there?"

"I'm here. We should talk about that, but not over the phone."

"Are you upset?" Jannika asked.

"I think today has been full enough for both of us. I'd like to bring over some soup for you if you want."

Jannika couldn't figure out why Lee might be upset. Maybe she was upset because she'd left and messed up their date or she didn't text Lee from the hospital? That seemed a little high maintenance. Maybe they were moving too fast.

"I'm pretty tired. I think I'm going to veg out on the couch for a while."

"Are you sure?"

"Yes, I'm sure."

"I'll call you tomorrow?"

"Sure, sounds good." Jannika ended the call and reread the message from Joanne.

Chapter Thirteen

Jannika's hands shook as she typed a reply to Joanne's text. She dropped the phone on the couch and plopped down beside it. She put her head in her hands and her shoulders shook as she tried to hold in the warring emotional factions—the dream date she had with Lee, and her feelings of betrayal talking with Joanne. She wanted to get on with her life. That's why she'd moved to New Hampshire. And she wanted to move on from Joanne. Maybe a part of her wanted Joanne to hurt the way she did. Maybe part of her wanted Joanne to realize what she had given up when she kicked Jannika out of the house and out of her life.

She woke to a dark house. The sun had long since set and her stomach told her it was way past dinnertime. She picked up her phone. Nothing else from Joanne, good. And nothing from Lee either.

She grabbed some of the leftover Chinese food from the other night and popped it in the microwave, then sent a text to Marcy. She hadn't heard much from Marcy lately since she and Amy were seeing each other. They went away a lot to avoid being seen together in Grangeton.

What's up, kiddo? Marcy texted.

Got a message today. Joanne is selling the house and found some of my stuff.

Oh, Marcy replied.

Wants me to come up.

Amy and I are at her place. You want me to come over?

Was it selfish of her, wanting Marcy to leave her girlfriend to listen to her problems? *I'm a mess. Gunnie is okay but was in the hospital today. Low blood sugar they think.*

Messy doesn't bother me. I'll be right over. About half an hour.

Jannika walked around the cottage, randomly picking up things then putting them down. She threw some laundry in the washing machine but didn't turn it on. She put on the kettle for tea and set out two mugs, a jar of honey, some lemon slices from the fridge, and some milk. She didn't know how Marcy or anyone else on earth could put milk in a nice cup of tea. The thought made her shudder. As the kettle was heating up, she went in the bathroom, washed her face, and tried to do something with the left side of her hair, which was now smashed into the side of her head at all angles from sleeping on the couch.

She scrubbed the kitchen counters and heard a car in the driveway. She threw the sponge in the sink, washed her hands, and opened the door at the first knock.

"Oh, Nick," Marcy said and wrapped her arms around her. "First, how is Gunnie?"

"She's okay. Scared me, though, to see her like that. They said she doesn't have diabetes, but she might be hypoglycemic. I took her home, got her settled in, and she seemed more like herself."

"Good. That must have scared the pants off you. Where were you?" Marcy asked.

Jannika plopped on the couch. "I was over at Lee's. We'd gone apple picking, and she brought me to her house to show me around," she said. "I got a call from Carol, Auntie's friend, to come to the hospital. While I was there, I got a text and a voicemail from Joanne that she and her girlfriend are selling the house." Jannika rubbed the back of her neck. Her jaw was set.

"Later, Aunt Gunnie told me she heard the same gossip I heard about Joe Bosworth being bored with the bookstore. I'm trying not to panic."

Marcy sat on the couch next to Jannika and turned to face her. "Do not panic. You know how Carol, and Gunnie, and all those ladies are. I think you need to call Joe and hear whatever it is he has to say about the store."

"Edgar told me to call Joe and ask him about the store too, when I saw him at the Simon's weekend."

"Don't you want to know?"

"You're right. I'm going to call him and find out what's up with the store, if anything." Jannika knew everyone was right, she should call her boss, but she was afraid of his answers. She didn't usually put off things like this, but she just wanted to pretend the rest of her life was stable and enjoy going out with Lee. "Do you want some tea or anything?"

"Like you have anything in your fridge besides frozen stuff. I'm okay. And now from left field—let's take a break from the heavy stuff and you can tell me about apple picking." Marcy scrunched a pillow behind her and leaned back against the couch.

Jannika's face relaxed, and she unfolded her legs.

"It was the best apple picking day." Jannika shook her head. "But I had to leave when I got the call about Auntie. It's probably just as well. I don't know what I'm feeling. I feel so comfortable with her and she is so…incredible. I've never had anyone look at me like she does. But do I want to take the chance of getting my heart broken? Look what happened with Joanne. I trusted her and you know how that ended. And now, out of the blue, she gets in touch. But I think I could finally get closure on the Joanne stuff if I go up to get the rest of *my* stuff. But I don't know if I can do it."

"Jannika, I have a proposition for you," Marcy said.

"What's that?" Jannika asked.

"I want to make a deal with you. I've told you how I feel about Amy," Marcy said.

"And I'm so, so happy for you—both of you, you know that," she said.

"I wanted you to know that I finally agree with you. There is a big block of something holding back my relationship with Amy. And it's labeled *parents*. I've decided to come out to my mother, then my father. But my mother first. Next weekend. Here's my deal. I think you and I both know you have unfinished business with Joanne, and that might, just might, be holding you back from your happiness. I think we should make a deal to do it this weekend. I'll come out to my mother and you take the trip to Maine and see Joanne. We can be brave for each other, you know? Hold each other up and all that stuff you always say to me when you're acting all Super Lesbian," Marcy said, putting her hand on Jannika's shoulder.

"I don't know if I can this weekend. I texted and told her I would come up, but I don't know…" Jannika said. "I'm not good at confrontation. I get really anxious."

"I know what you've told me about Lee. And you can tap dance all around it, but you really like this woman. I see it in your face when you talk about her. Would you want to move forward with someone who seems still hung up on their ex?"

"Kind of harsh," she said.

"Kind of true," Marcy said.

"I never compared our situations before. You're right, as usual. But I don't know. Part of me is still hurt, and part of me is angry at the way she treated me," Jannika said. She ran her hand through her hair, then over the back of her neck. Her stomach churned at the thought of confronting Joanne. "I don't know what to do."

"Yes, you do." Marcy sat up and put her hand on Jannika's knee and looked her in the eye.

"Okay, I'll do it," Jannika said.

"Next weekend, right?"

"Next weekend."

"And you'll call Lee and let her know what's going on. Don't leave her in the dark," Marcy said.

"She's calling me tomorrow," Jannika said. "And you and I will check in with each other Sunday night. I'll text you or you text me."

"You got it." Marcy gave her a hug. "She's something, your camp counselor, huh?"

"Yes, she's something." Jannika smiled and thought about their afternoon before the phone call about her aunt. She was running up the stairs behind Lee—

"I wish you could see the look on your face right now. Ooh la la. I've never seen you like this. It's flippin' awesome. Just so you know."

"Thanks, you." She poked Marcy in the upper arm.

"Welcome," said Marcy. "I'm gonna get going. I'll leave you to your wild and luscious thoughts about the camp counselor. We can do this." She gave Jannika a hug.

"Very funny. Yes, we can."

She shut the door to the cottage. She picked up her phone from the coffee table and thought about texting Lee but decided that she wanted Lee to hear her voice. She looked at the time on her phone. It was too late to call tonight. she'd call first thing in the morning.

Chapter Fourteen

H ey, Jannika."
"Hey." Lee had answered the phone after the first ring. "I know you said you wanted to talk about something, and I need to talk about something too."

"Can we talk in person? I haven't had my breakfast yet, have you? Do you go into work today?" Lee asked.

"No breakfast. No work. I stay home on a Monday every once in a while, to catch up on paperwork. Sarah's at the store. I wanted to call you first thing."

"How about I bring over some breakfast and coffee or tea if that's okay, or you could come here?" Lee asked.

"Why don't you come over here," Jannika said. "I'll give you directions."

Jannika told Lee how to get to her cottage, then ran around and straightened things that didn't need straightening. She had already taken a shower and dressed in jeans, a white T-shirt, and a gray V-necked sweater. The cottage was in pretty good shape after her cleaning frenzy last night waiting for Marcy to get there. She moved her toaster oven over about three inches, then moved the big blue pottery bowl on the kitchen counter to the coffee table. Then she moved it back to its original place. She opened her bedroom door, then had second thoughts and closed the bedroom door. She checked to see if she had clean towels in the bathroom, reaching up every now and then to rub the back of her neck. She started a grocery list. She turned music on, then she turned it off. She got out some orange Fiestaware dinner plates, a couple of forks and knives, and two orange and red striped placemats. Then she stood in the middle of the living room, looked out the sliding glass doors, and took a deep breath. Lee's truck rolled toward the house, down the driveway. Her stomach did several backflips.

She watched Lee get out of her car and reach back in for a white paper bag and a cardboard cup carrier holding two large cups. She let Lee and her packages into the cottage. Lee set the food and drink on the kitchen table, then pulled Jannika into her arms.

"I am so happy to be here," Lee said.

"Me too." Jannika felt a catch in her throat.

Lee looked around the small cottage. "This is a great place. It fits you, cozy and neat with a little old-fashioned charm thrown in for good measure," Lee said. She reached in the bag and removed foodstuffs wrapped in white butcher's paper.

"You make me sound like a quilt my auntie would have made," Jannika said. She frowned. She didn't want Lee to see her as some straitlaced, single-for-way-too-long person.

"I listed a few of your surface qualities. I know that under that cozy exterior beats the heart of a wild woman," Lee said. She smiled at Jannika.

Jannika felt her ears grow warm. When Lee smiled at her like that, whatever she wanted to talk about slipped away, and everything faded except Lee, standing next to her. She didn't feel cozy at all. She felt like she wanted to take Lee in the other room and ravish her.

"I picked up a couple of Portuguese breakfast roll sandwiches from TJ's. They have local ham, egg, and cheddar cheese in them. Lots of protein and some very yummy tasting carbs to boot. Oh, and when I left my house, I swung by the orchard and picked up a couple of cider doughnuts."

Jannika tried to focus on what Lee was saying and not on the effect Lee was having on her body. "Oh, Lee, that was so sweet and thoughtful. I'm sorry about yesterday. I want to talk about it."

"I do too, but let's get some food into us before we go digging around into what I'm sure is going to be emotional territory for both of us," Lee said. She unwrapped a sandwich and took a bite. "This is the best bite, try yours."

Jannika thought about how the events played out yesterday when she got the phone call about Aunt Gunnie. She thought it was a little overboard for Lee to be upset at the way she left her house in such a hurry—it was a family emergency after all—and she didn't know why that might be emotional territory, as Lee put it. She took a bite of her breakfast sandwich.

"Oh my God, how have I not known these existed? This is incredible," Jannika said. She covered her mouth with her hand after realizing that she was talking with a mouth full of food. "Sorry, I couldn't help myself."

It took them all of twenty minutes to finish their breakfast. They picked up the wrappers, plates, and forks and brought them into the kitchen. Jannika put hers on the counter and turned to take Lee's from her. As she took the plate from Lee she looked into her eyes.

"Come sit down with me. Marcy came over last night and she helped me a lot," Jannika said. She put Lee's plate in the sink, took her hand, and led her into the living room.

Jannika sat down and tucked herself into the corner by the arm of the couch. She angled herself so she faced Lee.

"Tell me about yesterday," Lee said. Her voice was soft and she reached out and put a hand on Jannika's folded leg.

"You know I got a call about Aunt Gunnie. And she's fine. I called her this morning before I called you and she feels *darn smart* today. I reminded her that she needed to call her doctor today and make an appointment. What I didn't tell you was that I got a text and voicemail from Joanne while I was at the hospital. Joanne and her girlfriend are selling the house and she found some of my stuff in the attic and wants me to come get it." She looked past Lee and out the French doors.

Her palms were moist. She rubbed them on her thighs. She looked at Lee. Beautiful, kind, sexy Lee. A big part of Jannika wanted to somehow skip this part, pretend she'd never gotten the text, and take Lee into the bedroom.

"And what does that mean to you?" Lee asked. She moved a little closer to Jannika.

"To be honest, part of me wants to forget I ever got that text. But I need to go up to Maine and talk to Joanne. It feels a little scary, because I don't like confrontation. But I've never had closure on that relationship, and I want to move forward in my life." She reached for Lee's hand. "I'm going up next weekend."

"I think that's very courageous," Lee said. "It sounds like it's the absolute right thing for you to do. I want to be honest with you too, Jannika. I hope that moving forward will mean moving forward with me, with us. And that might be coming on too strong and too fast, but there is something between us—I think you feel it too. It's more than our physical attraction. It's something deeper. Do you have a sense of that too?" Lee moved even closer to Jannika and put her right arm on the back of the couch.

"Yes," she said. "I felt it that first time we were walking back to the store and we went and got the cookies. And you are very close to me right now." Jannika smiled. She had to concentrate to get the words out. The proximity of her body to Lee's was too close for intellectual thought. Her body hummed with desire. She saw her desire reflected in Lee's eyes as well.

"Yes, I am very close to you, aren't I?" Lee said. She drew herself even closer and slipped her arm around Jannika's waist. She brought her lips to meet Jannika's.

She wrapped her arms around Lee's neck. Lee's kiss wasn't just a kiss—it was a promise. Jannika opened herself to accept what Lee was giving. She felt her eyes fill and her heart beat faster. She wanted to be able to give Lee the same promise.

Lee ended the kiss by stroking Jannika's cheek with the back of her hand. She sat back against the couch cushion. "You are so beautiful." She traced Jannika's hairline across her forehead, down her temple, and behind her left ear.

"And you are incredible," Jannika said. "That kiss…was…I don't have words." She reached over and took Lee's hand in hers.

"I understand why you need to go to Maine. I love that you're being honest, with yourself and with me. I need to talk to you about something too," Lee said. She squeezed Jannika's hand and ran her thumb up and down over the back of her knuckles.

"What?" Jannika asked. She felt her stomach grow tight when she saw the look on Lee's face.

"I want to tell you a little about Shannon's death to help you understand something about me," Lee said, reaching over and clasping Jannika's free hand.

"Of course. I want to hear whatever you want to say," Jannika said, both her hands now held by Lee.

"You may not want to hear this, but I need to say this. I told you that Shannon was killed in a car accident, but I didn't tell you what kind of car accident. Shannon was killed by a man who was going too fast around a corner. He lost control of his car and plowed into Shannon's car. The force of the impact flipped her car over an embankment," Lee said. She pulled one of her hands away and rubbed her forehead.

"Oh my God," Jannika said. She bit her lower lip. "That's awful, horrible. I'm so sorry, Lee."

"The driver broke his legs and his back, but he lived. He said he was just fooling around. He was very sorry." Lee's jaw was set and her words came out hard and flat. "Yesterday when you got that call about your aunt, you peeled out of my driveway. I felt sick inside after you left."

That explained the weird tone of their phone call. "I'm sorry I left like that. I understand now how that would upset you," Jannika said. She was also kind of embarrassed. The last thing she wanted to do was anything that would hurt Lee.

"I was pissed at the way you drove off. Totally pissed. There aren't too many things that I come down hard on, but speeding is probably number one. Tell me that isn't a habit of yours, that it was a one-time thing," Lee said. Her face was pale and tight.

"It wasn't a one-time thing," Jannika said.

"It isn't?" Lee asked. Her voice was low and soft.

Jannika tried to look anywhere but at Lee's face. She didn't want to lie to Lee ever, but the truth was going to be hard to say.

"It's a bad habit of mine. When I'm upset I tend to speed. Marcy and my Aunt Gunnie are always on me about it—"

"They should be on you about it. Damn it, Jannika. Do you want to kill somebody?"

"Of course I don't want to kill anyone. That's an awful thing to say," Jannika said.

"Before you go to Maine, you need to know that as much as I truly want to see where this goes with you and how much I want to be with you, I can't—no, I won't be afraid of getting you upset because you'll go speeding off someplace. Or worrying that someone else will piss you off and you'll go off speeding and either get yourself killed or kill someone's mother or lover or daughter," Lee said. Her eyes were filled. As she blinked they overflowed and tears ran down her face. "I won't. I can't."

Lee turned away, her face in her hands.

Jannika's heart felt like it would jump right out of her chest. She looked at the woman sitting next to her on her couch and uncurled her legs. She moved next to Lee and ran her hand up Lee's back. Her heart was still pounding.

"I'm so sorry. I'll try not to speed." She continued to rub Lee's back with a sweaty palm. She didn't know what else to do.

Lee took Jannika's hands in hers. "My brain knows that you're going to try, and my heart wants to believe it, but speeding just sets me off. It's like I poured all my grief and loss into the speeding, so that I could get through the everyday things. I know it probably sounds over the top or irrational even, but if you care about me, please don't speed."

"I don't want to ever cause you worry or pain. I know I probably will at some time, but not over something I can control. Will you help me? It's a habit I've had for a long, long time and it might be hard to break. But I promise you that I will try to never speed in the car again," Jannika said. She swallowed the lump of fear that rose in her throat when she thought about losing Lee after just finding her again. Her friends and family had chastised her about her bad habit for years, but their worry and fear never reached inside of her the way Lee's did.

"There's something else," Lee said looking into Jannika's eyes.

"What?"

"I want to tell you the rest of the story around Shannon's accident."

"Absolutely." Jannika's stomach was in knots. She held Lee's hands. Every word that Lee said mattered to her.

"The day of the accident was like any other day. I wasn't in the greatest of moods and Shannon wanted me to go to the store. I was angry because I always did the errands, and I said so. Shannon grabbed her bag and her keys and I can still hear her say what she said as she slammed out the door. They were her last words to me. *Sometimes you suck, darling.* And that was it. An hour later I got the call. Even after all this time and some pretty heavy-duty therapy, I still think it should have been me. And things like this just trigger those memories and my guilt." Tears formed at the edges of Lee's eyes.

She leaned forward, took Lee's face into her hands, and placed gentle kisses around her eyes and on her cheeks. Then she smoothed the hair from Lee's forehead and kissed there and touched her forehead to Lee's. They sat like that for a moment, and then she wrapped her arms around Lee, and Lee wrapped her arms around her waist and leaned her head on her shoulder.

Chapter Fifteen

Jannika left New Hampshire midafternoon on Sunday and headed to Maine to see Joanne. I-95 north bottlenecked about five miles after the Piscataqua River Bridge, as Jannika passed the exit for York and Ogunquit. Traffic was heavy on Fridays and Saturdays, with everyone from Massachusetts traveling north or going to the coast, but Sundays were usually traffic free. She touched the front left pocket of her jeans and felt the small hard outline of a stone. Marcy had stopped by before she left and picked up a stone from Jannika's driveway and pressed it against her heart. She told Jannika that when she felt afraid or nervous in Maine or like she couldn't go through with it, touch the stone. Jannika had picked up a stone, pressed it against her heart, and given it to Marcy. Marcy had jokingly called them their touchstones.

She reached into her snack bag for some of the fluffernackers she'd packed. Uncle Charlie had introduced her to the treat, with peanut butter on one cracker and marshmallow fluff on another, stuck together like a mini fluffernutter sandwich. Jannika called them fluffernackers when she was around three years old, and they'd been fluffernackers ever since. Aunt Gunnie couldn't believe she still ate them.

After thirty minutes of crawling, the cars started to move ahead faster. Jannika looked out the passenger window at the remnants of an accident and hoped that no one was hurt badly. She thought of the conversation she'd had with Lee a few days ago. She couldn't imagine losing someone she loved in such a violent way.

Jannika drove directly to Maine Medical Center in Portland. She hoped that Joanne still worked the weekend shift. She parked in the parking garage and took the elevator to the second floor. The sound of her heart beating muffled the conversations happening around her.

She saw Joanne at a desk in one of the seven outpatient registration cubes. The memory of Joanne's betrayal only made her feel stronger. Her confidence grew as she walked closer to Joanne's cubicle. There was no one in line, so she went straight to Joanne's desk.

"Are you kidding me, Jannika? You pick now to show up, just show up?"

"You said as soon as possible." Jannika shoved her trembling hands into her pockets.

"Did it cross your mind to call or text?"

"I'm here today and I've borrowed a truck." She fingered the stone in her pocket and it gave her another burst of confidence. She realized that Joanne and the memory of their relationship no longer had a hold on her heart. She just wanted to get her things and get back home to Lee.

"I get out in a few minutes, but I have things I have to do. Meet me at the house at seven."

"At seven?" Jannika said.

"Tough shit, Nick, meet me at the house at seven, or forget about your stuff. You're really rude, you know, just showing up like this. I'll make sure Lucy doesn't pop over—that would be inconvenient, wouldn't it?"

"Is Lucy your…"

"Yes, she's my lover." Joanne thrust her chin in the air. "I can't talk here. Meet me at seven at the house."

A CHAPTER ON LOVE

Jannika nodded and rode the elevator down to her car. She didn't like confrontation, but she felt like she was taking back part of her life and making it her story. Not someone else's story. She'd come face-to-face with the person who broke her heart and betrayed her. She used to think about that moment and what she would do, what she would say.

Now she had two hours to kill, and as she drove to the mall near the hospital, she considered how to spend that time. She still had friends here, but she didn't want to see any of the old crowd she and Joanne used to hang around with. But she also didn't want to sit in her car in the mall parking lot for two hours. It was a cold, gray November day with a raw east wind off the ocean. Not a good day for walking around town. She picked up her phone and made a call.

"Edgar Goodale here."

"Hi, Edgar, it's Jannika."

"To what do I owe the gift of this good fortune?" Edgar said.

She explained the Joanne situation. "But I can't go over till seven. I'm in the mall parking lot."

"Come over and see me, my friend. I have an interesting item that came in a week or so ago. I think you might like to see it. This is fortuitous, Jannika," Edgar said.

"For both of us." She chuckled. Edgar's voice was as soothing as a warm cup of tea. "See you in fifteen minutes or so," she said.

Jannika drove to Goodale Books, pulled into the narrow alleyway between the bookstore and the Galley Restaurant, and parked in her old space behind the store. She breathed a sigh of familiarity. So much had happened in her life since her time working at Edgar's store. Edgar and Helen had been so much a part of her life after she left her mother's house to come down to college in Portland. Edgar's shop and his home felt more like home than her mother's house ever did.

She had learned how to buy new books when she worked at Barnes and Noble, but Edgar taught her about used books, old books, how a book was made, and how to do simple repairs to a treasured book. The first year, all Edgar let her do was arrange books on the shelves, cash out customers, and watch him. And learn.

Then one day, she'd helped a customer when Edgar was busy in the back room. She thought he'd been out of earshot, but his reaction surprised her and the words he'd said set the course for her professional life. *That, my dear, was the most stunning display of reader's advisory I've witnessed. You have a remarkable intuitive connection with our customers. Don't be stingy with it.*

From that day on, they'd become more like partners in the store. Outside of the store, Edgar and Helen welcomed her into their home like the daughter they never had.

Edgar opened the rear door and waved her in. "Let me give you the grand tour of your old stomping ground." He showed Jannika how he had rearranged the store and some of his latest finds.

Then he crouched behind the tall wood counter and brought out a small box. "Now lay your eyes on this."

He lifted off the cover of the box and Jannika looked inside at an old book.

"Whoa, that's a once in a lifetime treasure. It's gorgeous. Where'd you find it?"

"Believe it or not, my lovely lady found it at a yard sale."

"Can I hold it?"

"Yes, of course. I'm sending this one out for repair by someone with more expertise than I. There are times one needs to take things apart in order to make them whole again." Edgar caught Jannika's eye.

"You're a wise man, Edgar Goodale. Let me wash my hands." She stepped into the small bathroom behind the counter that was the size of a broom closet. Indeed, it had been a broom closet before Edgar put in the bathroom.

"She must be a splendid someone for you to come back to see *her*." Edgar wrinkled his nose.

"Yes, she is splendid." Jannika smiled at the thought of Lee as she pulled a sheet of paper from the big roll under the counter and placed it on the table next to the counter. She placed the book on the paper and carefully examined it, then put it back in its box. "Shouldn't you have that under lock and key?"

"No one knows about it yet. But I'm sure there will be solicitations soon."

Edgar continued to show Jannika his latest finds, and she filled him in on The Pageturner.

And now it was time to face Joanne. "Well, thanks for the distraction, and what a treat to see you twice in one month. I thought I'd feel more on edge coming to the house again, but I'm glad she called. I need to—as you'd say—have a proper good-bye."

Edgar put his arm around Jannika's shoulder as they walked to the door.

"I want you to look at her when you see her. Really look at her. Not as you remember her, not as you want her to be. Just as she is. You have an honorable heart, my dear. Follow where it leads."

"Thank you." She kissed him on his cheek. "I'll drop you an email later this week."

Jannika drove to Joanne's house in silence, reaching into her bag to eat more fluffernackers for fortification and gulping tea from a thermos Edgar filled at the store. She pulled behind a white Subaru Legacy and felt her pocket for the touchstone. *You can do this, Nick.* She heard Marcy's words in her head.

Joanne opened the door as Jannika hit the second stair on the porch. She had changed after work. Her choice of attire for this meeting was a very tight white tank top and skintight black jeans.

"A little cool for a tank top, don't you think?" Jannika said. She walked past Joanne and headed for the living room. Her head spun as she looked around. It was her first time in the house, their house, since the night they broke up. The night Joanne kicked her out and never wanted to see her or speak to her again. She put her hand on the seat of a barstool to steady herself. Everywhere she looked were memories. Joanne had changed nothing.

"You noticed?" Joanne said. She looked down at her chest, then at Jannika.

Joanne's nipples were a distraction she didn't need right now.

"The boxes are over there." Joanne pointed to a hallway off the living room. "Take them out, and I'll make sure there's nothing else you left here."

"I didn't *leave* anything. You kicked me out and had your friends bring me my stuff. In garbage bags."

"You were always so fucking sensitive." Joanne looked at Jannika like she was making a decision about something, then walked into the hallway off the living room. "It's only five boxes, Nick. I thought there was one more with some of your precious books."

Jannika opened the front door and propped open the wooden screen door with the brick they had always left on the top step for that purpose. Her ears rang with the familiarity of everything. She brought a box to the truck and balanced it on her hip as she flipped the tailgate down with one hand. Lee had offered to let her use her Toyota, but that didn't feel right, and she borrowed Hannah's truck instead.

Joanne dropped a small box in the doorway. She turned and went back into the house. Jannika finished loading the truck and went back inside. She moved the brick with her foot and let the screen door shut behind her.

"I want to talk about us, about why you never answered my calls or my texts. Why your friends had to bring me my stuff.

Why I couldn't come back in my house and talk to you about what you did. To us."

"It's my house, Nick, remember? You didn't want your name on the mortgage. It felt like too much of a commitment to you, too fast, you said. Remember? And remember how you screwed me over? You told me that you were leaving straight from work to go to your mother's for the weekend."

Jannika wanted to say everything she hadn't gotten a chance to say when Joanne ordered her out of their house. "I screwed you over? I decided to stay home with you that weekend, and when I came home you were in bed with your ex. Our bed. In our house. And you screamed at me to get out like I was the intruder." She crossed her arms over her chest.

"Did you ever try to come to the house, Nick? In all this time, did you ever try to fight for me? No, I didn't want to talk to you on the phone or text you, damn you, I wanted you to come back for me, show me that I mattered to you, but no, you ran away. You ran clean out of state. Fuck you, Nick." Joanne's face was flushed and she gave Jannika the finger. "Fuck you."

Mind. Blown. "I was trying to respect your wishes, and I was hurt. You broke my heart."

"You were chicken." A bit of spit flew out of Joanne's mouth and landed on Jannika's cheek.

She took a deep breath, gathered herself, and said, "You cheated on me and I didn't deserve that. No one deserves to be treated that way. I'm glad you called. Thanks for my stuff. So long, Joanne." Jannika walked toward the door. Her heart was pounding, but she felt good. She felt powerful.

As she stepped over the threshold of Joanne's house and into the crisp November night, she felt a little shaky on the outside, but on the inside, her heart put its hands on its hips. She patted her pocket where her stone sat.

CHAPTER SIXTEEN

Lee grabbed a hanger with a tan park shirt and another with the green pants that completed her uniform. Her boss had called an off-season Monday meeting, and her wrinkled clothes hung in the closet where she'd put them when she unpacked a couple of months ago. She ironed her uniform, using the tip of the iron on her State of New Hampshire State Parks patch and the small bar below, her manager patch. She should be reviewing her initial assessment notes for her park, but instead her mind was busy planning all the things she wanted to do with Jannika.

She found a tie and belt and was all set. It was warm for early November, so she grabbed a light jacket and headed out. Halfway to Concord, she stopped for gas and a black coffee. She'd had a great time over the weekend visiting with her sister and her parents. She helped the kids make a scarecrow woman with some of her mother's old clothes and piles of leaves they raked. But she was glad when she saw the text from her boss about the morning meeting, and she left her sister's on Sunday afternoon. She loved her new park.

Watts Lake State Park was one of the smaller parks in New Hampshire. There were fifteen campsites, two group camping areas, and a day use area near the beach. The park office had a small apartment upstairs which she could've used during the season for free and found a rental just for the winter, but it was too small, and anyway, she fell in love with the farm the first time she saw it. She'd spent the better part of September getting to know the park and the staff. Her predecessor stayed on until the end of the season to show her around, to teach her the park's individual quirks and personality.

But now, she had four months off work, November through February. The downtime fed her introverted side. All summer she was the go-to person for every problem at the park. Since Shannon had passed away, she'd spent the winters doing some admin work a few days a week and worked on her carvings and other projects the rest of the time. This was her routine, and it fit her well. Comfortable, like an old pair of sweatpants and favorite camp T-shirt. She was hoping to work out a similar off-season schedule here, and this meeting would be a chance to discuss it with her boss. She was glad to have something to do instead of waiting around to hear how Jannika's visit with her ex turned out.

She merged onto I-93. Bumper to bumper as far as she could see. She fingered her state issued ID and lanyard and remembered another lanyard eighteen years ago and a tall, striking girl with blond hair.

Lee was pulling in after a solo sunset canoe trip around the pond at Camp Pine Knoll. As she dragged her green canoe out of the water, she saw Jannika sitting with her back against a big old white pine. Her long tanned legs were stretched out straight in front of her, and Day-Glo green flip flops sat beside them. Jannika was running her thumb along the inside of the ID lanyard she wore around her neck.

Lee asked, "Hey, Jannika, why aren't you at the rec hall watching the movie?"

Jannika walked up to her and slowly took the lanyard off her neck and put it around Lee's. "You must have dropped this—I was keeping it safe for you," she said. Then she tilted her head slightly, bit her bottom lip, and took off into the pines.

Lee had spent years in Girl Scout camps and everyone knew younger girls had crushes on older girls. But nothing had prepared her for Jannika Peterson during her final summer as a camp counselor. Lee wasn't sure she was any better prepared now, eighteen years later. Those years had fine-tuned Jannika's beauty and turned cute into incredibly sexy.

The parking lot at the state building was almost full. Lee was happy to have a small truck as she maneuvered into a tight space. She was halfway across the lot when her phone vibrated.

Hey there. I'm back. Got in late last night. Lots to talk about.

Lee didn't know if that was good news or bad news. Her stomach tightened as she texted back. *Good to hear from you. Headed into a meeting in Concord. Talk later?*

Call me tonight. I'll be home after six. I can't wait to see you.

K

Lee turned off her phone for the meeting. This could turn out to be one of the best days of her life.

❖

Jannika put her phone down. Still no word from Marcy about how her weekend went. She was getting worried.

She made some toast and tea for breakfast, plugged her phone into her speakers, and chose a New Age playlist. Sarah never ran out of suggestions for stress reducing music, herbs, and essential oils. Marcy's face appeared on the screen as she was adjusting the volume. She pulled the jack from the phone and tapped Marcy's image.

"I waited all night for you to call me, you booger," Marcy said.

"I was waiting for you."

"We suck," Marcy said.

"Yes, we suck, and yes, I did it. It was hard and wonderful. I felt…I feel like I took a piece of me back. Did you see your mom?"

"I did and it was great. She was great. I was nervous, shit, I was *nervous*. I kept touching that damn stone."

"Me too. Tell me."

"I told her. She suspected. I kind of got pissed because she suspected and never said anything. She got all teary and I started to panic, but she thought I was sick or I'd gotten into some kind of trouble or something. She felt bad for not being there for me. I started to get pissed again about that, because she never seemed open to hearing about me. But then I thought about Amy and how I want to have a regular life. I know I'm supposed to give my mom space to adjust and all that stuff, but I couldn't help myself and I told her about Amy."

"Marce, that's amazing. How did she react?"

"She looked kinda gobsmacked, but put up a good front. She was really trying. I think we can be close again. It felt like when I was a kid, and she was there for me. Always in my corner. It felt like that." Marcy sniffed.

"Oh, Marce. I'm so happy for you. I've got goose bumps. And I'm so proud of you for being so brave. And wow, that's huge."

"Thanks. More about me later. And you? And Joanne?"

"I stopped to see Edgar first. He was great, as always. He had a find to show me. You should've seen it. It was—"

"Nick. Hello, Nick? Joanne?"

"Sorry. I went to the hospital first, then met her at the house later. She tried to somehow make the breakup my fault, but I said what I needed to say. I was shaking inside, but it felt really good after I said it and drove away. It feels finished."

"And then there's Lee," Marcy said.

"And then there's Lee. I love that you're my friend." Jannika sat back on the couch and bumped her husky-dog slippers together. "I texted her this morning and she's calling me tonight. What about you?"

"She's calling you, you knucklehead? Invite her over or go over to her house. We're both past the age of playing hard to get.

I'm driving to the South Shore to go over financials with one of the restaurants. Next weekend my mom is planning a dinner at the house and I'm going to do it all over again with my dad. I'll have my mom right there, so it doesn't feel as scary. I've got this crazy dream that we'll all be together at this big old wedding someday soon."

Jannika stood up and bumped the coffee table, spilling tea on an issue of *Publishers Weekly*. "What? What wedding? Whose wedding?"

"I haven't told anyone. Amy and I haven't talked about marriage, but she's it. She's the one, I feel it. When I'm on the road, all I think about it my future with her, what we'll be doing in three years, ten years, twenty years. I see us at our wedding, and I see my parents there, both of them." Marcy whispered, "I've never felt this way about anyone, Nick. Never."

"I'm so happy for you, but isn't this kind of fast, even by lesbian standards?"

"Maybe, but I don't care. I haven't asked her yet. I want everything with my parents to be sorted out. I'll let you—"

Marcy's phone cut out. She must have hit the tunnel. Jannika hung up and waited a few minutes, but Marcy didn't call back. She was happy for her, but she and Amy had been seeing each other for only a few weeks, and the jump to marriage seemed like an Olympic leap. She cleaned up her spill and left for the bookstore.

It turned out to be a very slow day, and Jannika left Sarah in charge and went home a couple of hours before closing. She got home and settled on the couch with an ARC from one of her favorite mystery writers.

❖

Jannika patted the coffee table in search of her phone which was ringing and vibrating. She didn't know what time it was, or what day it was, for that matter. Lee's number flashed on the screen. She must have fallen asleep.

"Hey." She rubbed the top of her head and sat up on the couch, willing her body to wake up. She removed her book from under her left thigh.

"Hey yourself."

"I was thinking, actually Marcy did the thinking for me today and suggested I tell you about what happened with Joanne in person, not over the phone, and she's right." Maybe a leap was sometimes necessary.

Lee said, "I was about to put dinner in the oven. Why don't you come over and I'll feed you."

"I love a woman who wants to feed me. Yes. I'll be there in an hour—not too late for dinner?"

"I can't wait to see you, Jannika."

"Me too. And Lee?"

"Yes?"

"Call me Nick."

Chapter Seventeen

The smell of baked apples and cinnamon greeted Jannika as Lee opened the door to the farmhouse. Lee looked into her eyes.

"Come on in, Nick." Lee smiled and opened the door wider.

Jannika's heart grew in her chest and her stomach fluttered. "I like the way you say that." She touched Lee's arm. Then it occurred to her that Lee was waiting, had been waiting, since she'd left for Maine. That's why her jaw looked so tight. Lee took her coat and hung it in the entryway.

"I roasted a chicken and some vegetables, and you probably smelled dessert on your way in. Apple pie. I made it with the apples we picked last week."

"Can the food wait a little while longer?"

"Sure, I just took the chicken and veggies out of the oven. Let me cover the chicken." Lee went into the kitchen.

Jannika followed Lee, then took her hand and stepped closer. They were inches apart. Jannika's heart pounded. Lee's steady gaze both grounded her and excited her.

"I finally feel like I have closure on that relationship. I wish I hadn't had to go to Maine to know that. But I did."

"Are you okay?" Lee stepped even closer to her.

"Sort of emotionally drained but excited at the same time, if that makes sense. And I felt the urge to let out some of my emotion through my driving, but I didn't. I drove safely. It was important that I tell you that. I missed you." She couldn't tell whose palm was getting sweaty, hers or Lee's.

"I'm glad you went to Maine, and thank you for telling me about the driving. I'd be lying if I said I wasn't concerned about that. I missed you too."

Jannika saw the color rise on Lee's cheeks and felt her face grow warm as well. "I think you should put the chicken in the fridge."

"You do?"

"Yes, I do." She took one more step and their lips met. Their kiss was slow and hungry. She felt the tip of Lee's tongue part her lips and her tongue answered back.

Jannika's hand ran through Lee's hair and up the back of her neck, caressing it and pulling Lee closer. Lee wrapped her arms around Jannika and her hands moved up Jannika's back and slowly made their way down again to her waist. They lingered at the small of her back, moving in slow, small circles as they kissed. The tips of her fingers slid beneath the waistband of Jannika's jeans.

"Chicken." Jannika stepped away from Lee. She was breathless and her clothes felt too tight as every part of her body longed for Lee's touch.

Lee opened the refrigerator door and held it open with her leg while she reached for the roasting pan.

"Let me help." Jannika took a couple of potholders from hooks on the wall near the stove, grabbed the roasting pan, and put in on the bottom shelf of the fridge.

"Now forget the damn chicken." Lee swooped an arm around Jannika's waist again and ran hot kisses along her collarbone and up the side of her neck. Her tongue found Jannika's ear, and she ran the tip of it along the outside curve.

Jannika moaned and her knees threatened to buckle. Lee held on tighter as they stumbled through the kitchen on their way to the living room, kicking off shoes, knocking a bunch of bananas off the kitchen counter, and rolling along the hallway walls, kissing. Lee's back was against the hallway wall and Jannika's hands crept under her T-shirt.

"Nick."

Jannika felt Lee's hot breath on her neck and Lee kissed her again and they turned. Now Jannika's back was against the wall. Lee's body pressed against her and part of Jannika couldn't believe this was happening. How many years' worth of Leslie fantasies had she stored up? And here she was with Leslie—no, with *Lee*, beautiful, sexy Lee, who wanted her as much as she wanted her.

They made it to the doorway of the living room and tried to make it to the couch. Lee pushed the coffee table out of the way with her foot and grabbed a throw blanket off the arm of the couch with one hand and held Jannika's hand with the other. Jannika started to unbutton her shirt and Lee stopped her.

Lee looked at Jannika with eyes filled with desire. "I want you in my bed. Can you make it upstairs?" Her voice was husky and low.

Jannika saw a look of concern mix with the fire in Lee's eyes. The look caused her stomach to contract and she caught her breath as she nodded her consent. "Yes."

Lee slid an arm around her waist and led her up the stairs to her bedroom.

They stood next to the old pineapple four-poster bed and Jannika once again started to unbutton her shirt. Lee gently wrapped her fingers around Jannika's.

"Let me." Lee kissed each of her fingers before releasing them, then kissed her lightly on her cheek, her jawline, and her neck. The kisses moved to the hollow at the base of her collarbone and inside the collar of her shirt. Lee ran the tip of her finger along Jannika's collarbone, down the edge of her shirt to the first button.

Jannika's lips parted and she hummed a low moan. Her back arched toward Lee.

Lee placed a lingering kiss above each button as she unbuttoned it. Her lips traced a line along Jannika's skin to the next button and Jannika felt Lee's hot breath on her skin. Lee unbuttoned the second button with a kiss, then the third and the fourth. Jannika's hands ran through Lee's hair as her back arched and her knees wobbled.

"Lee." Jannika was having a hard time speaking and standing up. As if Lee read her mind, she unbuttoned the final button, slid the shirt over Jannika's shoulders, and reached around to unfasten her bra.

"You are so beautiful." Lee's gaze traveled over Jannika.

Jannika felt beautiful, desirable, and strong under Lee's gaze. She grabbed hold of the bottom of Lee's T-shirt and pulled it up and over Lee's head. Lee slid off her jeans and Jannika unzipped her own pants and started pulling them down. Lee took Jannika's hand and guided her down onto the bed as she kissed her. Lee then somehow managed to slide the rest of Jannika's clothes off her body. Jannika laughed. Lee crept back onto the bed, knees straddling Jannika's waist.

Any guardedness left Jannika as Lee gazed down at her.

Lee leaned over and kissed her lips, then followed her jawline with kisses. She paused and whispered in her ear as she slid her body on top of Jannika's. "I want to make love to you, Nick." Lee wrapped an arm around Jannika and they rolled onto their sides, facing each other.

Jannika felt Lee's words travel down her body like a caress.

They kissed while Lee's hand traced long lines down Jannika's back. Lee's kisses made their way to Jannika's neck again. The tip of Lee's tongue barely touched Jannika's skin as she kissed her way down to her breasts. The pulse between Jannika's legs grew stronger and her hips jerked as Lee's kisses met her breast. Lee moaned and the vibration of the moan ran through Jannika's body in a direct line to the wetness between her legs. Her back arched and Lee's mouth found Jannika's hard nipple. Lee gently held Jannika's hips and moved her from her side to her back. Lee's lips never lost contact with the nipple she caressed with her tongue. Lee caressed both breasts while her mouth worked Jannika's nipple.

"Lee, I…I'm…" Jannika panted and ground her hips into the bedcovers. She was trying to keep some kind of focus on her own hands touching Lee's firm back and shoulders. She moved her hands up to touch the sides of Lee's breasts just as Lee moved her kisses down Jannika's ribcage to her right hipbone. Her mind lost focus again and all thought left her head. She was immersed in her body's reactions to Lee touching, kissing, sucking, and moving her naked body on top of Jannika's nakedness. Lee's hard nipples made trails of sensation down Jannika's stomach and thighs as Lee slid down her body and kissed all around Jannika's hipbone.

Lee raised her head and looked up at Jannika whose neck was arched and face was full of desire.

"Hey, Nick."

"Mmmm." Jannika's hips flexed and her hands found Lee's face.

"I want you, Nick."

Jannika moaned.

"I wanted to make slow wonderful love to you, and I promise I will, but not right now. You're driving me crazy and I want to taste you and make you come. You're pretty close, aren't you?"

"Oh, Lee, yes. Yes, please." Jannika's hands gave Lee the signal to move lower and she parted her legs wider. She moaned again and her breath came in short gasps.

Lee's fingers drew a line along the inside of Jannika's left thigh and Jannika whimpered.

Lee slid first one, then two fingers inside Jannika.

"Oh my God, Nick." Lee's voice was husky and low. "You're so wet."

Jannika arched her back. "Please, Lee. Now. Now." Jannika's hands gripped the blankets and her head moved from side to side.

Lee moved her two fingers in and out of Jannika's wetness, exploring the feel of her. Jannika's hips began to pump in time with Lee's fingers. Lee withdrew her fingers and nuzzled her, moaning and exploring Jannika deeper with her tongue. She moved her tongue in and out of Jannika's wetness and Jannika spread her legs even wider. Lee found Jannika's clit with her tongue and spread her lips with two fingers, playing her tongue over Jannika's clit while Jannika moaned and thrashed beneath her.

Lee's hips began to jerk and she was wet and hot with desire.

Jannika grabbed wildly at the blankets. Her hips bucked. Lee slid two fingers into Jannika and Jannika's body became still and tense as she contracted around Lee's fingers.

Jannika growled a low moan as she came.

Lee's back arched and her thighs gripped together. She cried out. "Oh yes. You are so beautiful right now." Lee removed her fingers slowly and kissed the inside of Jannika's thigh.

"Come here," Jannika said as she tried to pull Lee up to her.

"I'm here." Lee moved onto her side to be next to Jannika.

"If you touch me again, I'll come," Jannika said.

Lee slid her thigh between Jannika's legs. "Let's see about that." Lee put her hand over Jannika's pussy, then curved her middle finger so it slipped easily inside.

Jannika groaned and pushed herself down onto Lee's hand.

Lee stroked in and out, curving her middle finger each time she pulled out.

Jannika gasped for air, opened her legs, and came hard while Lee held her.

Wetness coated the inside of Lee's thighs as her hips pumped wildly.

Jannika's left hand went in search of Lee's center, urging Lee to open her legs. Jannika's eyes never left Lee's as she slid one finger into her. "You are burning up."

Lee nodded.

"Let me fix that." Jannika slid two, then three fingers easily and moved them slowly in and out as Lee rocked on her hand.

Lee threw her head back and groaned.

Jannika moved her thigh closer to her hand that was working Lee. Lee's hand gripped Jannika's hip, moving in time with her thrusts. Jannika turned her fingers slightly as she moved them in and out.

"Oh, Nick, yes." Lee's voice broke as she panted and gasped for air, her hips grinding down into Jannika's hand and thigh.

Jannika kissed Lee's neck.

Lee's body relaxed and Jannika slowly removed her hand but kept her palm on Lee's mound. Jannika slid her thigh away a few inches and continued to kiss Lee's neck.

"Your hand." Lee's reply was a low growl.

"Hmm, what about my hand?" Jannika asked. "I'm not doing anything."

"I know and it's driving me crazy." Lee moved her hips back and forth.

"Stay still for a minute," Jannika said. She bent her head over Lee's breast and circled the nipple with her tongue. Lee's hips bucked. "Shh. Easy," Jannika whispered to Lee's breast.

"Oh my God, Jannika. I need to move."

"Just another minute." Jannika filled her mouth with breast, then slowly released Lee's breast up to the nipple which she kept in her mouth. She teased the nipple with the tip of her tongue and applied a little pressure to Lee's pussy with her other hand.

Lee flung her head back and small staccato moans filled the room.

Jannika sucked on Lee's nipple and slid a finger into Lee's wetness. Lee grabbed for the headboard with one hand and pushed against Jannika's hand as she came.

"That was amazing," Jannika said.

"Incredible." Lee wrapped her arms around Jannika and Jannika gave Lee a little pat, then caressed the small of Lee's back.

"Wonderful," Jannika whispered.

"Marvelous," Lee whispered back.

They kissed slow, relaxed kisses, exploring each other's bodies with the fascination of new lovers. Jannika jumped when Lee kissed her right knee.

"Sorry," Jannika said.

"Ticklish knees?" Lee propped herself up on one elbow alongside Jannika.

"Just one."

"Just one knee?" Lee asked.

"I know it's weird, but yes, just my right knee." Jannika rubbed her kneecap where Lee had kissed it. "Are you ticklish?"

"Yes," Lee said. "But I'm not going to tell you where. You're going to have to find out."

Jannika started pecking little kisses on Lee's forehead and cheek. "There? There?" She stopped and looked at Lee.

"You know, don't you, we just fulfilled about seven of my fantasies about making love with you," Jannika said.

"Seven? How many do you have?"

"Hundreds, maybe thousands." She bit her lip. "I'm hungry."

"So you have a ticklish right knee, you get hungry after sex, and you have hundreds of sex fantasies about me?"

"Thousands." Jannika grinned.

"Then let's feed you, and maybe you can share a few of those fantasies with me. There's some cold chicken and apple pie downstairs."

"Yum." Jannika jumped out of bed and threw on her shirt. "Let's go."

"And you jump out of bed after sex like the sheets are on fire."

Lee grabbed her pants and shirt and put them on as she followed Jannika down the hallway to the stairs. She stopped in the living room to put a couple of logs in the woodstove. "I don't want those beautiful long legs getting cold."

"I probably should have put my pants on."

"You never have to put pants on again, as far as I'm concerned."

Jannika loved the way Lee looked at her. She took the roasting pan out of the fridge and they stood at the kitchen counter ripping pieces of chicken off the bird.

"This is fantastic," Jannika said. "Do you like the skin? The crispy bits of skin are the best part. God, why does food always taste so good after sex?" Jannika popped a piece of skin in her mouth with greasy fingers.

Lee stepped closer. "Because after sex every nerve, every sense is heightened. Here, let me show you." Lee took Jannika's hand. "I believe you have some chicken grease still on your fingers." She licked the tip of each finger while she looked at Jannika. Then Lee turned her hand over and gently kissed the palm, making small circles with the tip of her tongue.

Jannika's knees buckled and a shiver zipped down her spine.

"You taste incredible. Hey, Nick." Lee grabbed Jannika and held her steady. She whispered in her ear, "When do I get to hear about the rest of those fantasies?"

"How does in five minutes sound?"

"Too long," Lee replied.

CHAPTER EIGHTEEN

The bright November sun woke Jannika and she stretched the full length of the bed. Or tried to. Her heels hit the footboard. "Crap. Work." She looked for a clock. "It's only eight." She breathed a sigh of relief and stretched her limbs again. Her body felt wonderful, her muscles were loose, and she wasn't sure she could describe how she felt. She felt...new. Her face grew warm as details of their night together floated through her mind and connected, making one steamy mind movie. They didn't get very much sleep last night. The sky was brightening when she'd finally closed her eyes, wrapped Lee's arm around her waist, and backed herself closer to Lee's warm body. But she felt rested. She felt better than she could ever remember feeling.

Her mind went back to those few long-ago weeks at Girl Scout camp. She'd had a girlfriend before that summer, but she'd never had the kind of all-consuming crush on anyone until she'd met Lee. She'd spent hours at camp thinking about and hoping that Lee would touch her or kiss her. Later, those thoughts and fantasies became more explicit. And now she was in Lee's bed and nothing she'd ever dreamed came close to the reality of them together.

And they might never have had this chance to be together if she hadn't, several years later, taken the advice Lee gave her at camp, the advice that gave her the strength to leave her mother's house. Lee was the first person to whom Jannika confessed her feeling of not being good enough, even as a baby, for her father to stick around. In the years since that summer, she'd worked through some of that with a few therapists. But the feeling of being not one hundred percent lovable dogged her until Lee came back into her life.

As she looked around the farmhouse bedroom and smelled coffee brewing, and heard either music playing or Lee singing, she thought she finally might be free. She was beginning to see herself through Lee's eyes. She threw on a robe Lee must have put at the foot of the bed and followed the coffee aroma to the kitchen. She looked around for Lee, but didn't see her.

The mudroom door opened and there stood a smiling rose-cheeked Lee. When their eyes met, Jannika knew she would remember the look on Lee's face this morning, for the rest of her life. She liked the sound of that, *the rest of her life*. Hope fluttered in her heart for the first time in a very long time.

"Hey, Nick."

"Hey yourself, beautiful."

"I wanted to let you sleep in—you looked so relaxed and peaceful. I got the stove running and water's hot for tea. I was fiddling with some things out in the barn."

"I wish I didn't have to go to work today, but Sarah's covered a lot of hours for me lately."

"Even though I'd love to have you all to myself today and continue what we started last night, I know you have a business to run. But I think we only covered a bare minimum of your fantasies." Lee held her and spoke the words into the base of her neck as she filled the spaces between her words with kisses.

"You can't do that and expect me to go to work." Jannika felt the deep beat of desire thrum in her body. Her hands traveled over Lee's back and into the curve of her lower back. She pulled her closer.

"I don't want to be anywhere but right here," Lee said. An internal video of the two of them together making many breakfasts and dinners in the farmhouse kitchen caught Lee off guard. She was used to taking relationships day by day ever since Shannon's death, and the future didn't factor in. Until now. She liked it but felt a touch of wariness. Having a future with someone also meant that future could be taken away.

"I don't want to go." Jannika took a deep breath. "But I have to."

"I'll make us some breakfast while you get ready for work, how does that sound?" Lee was finding it difficult to keep her hands busy and away from Nick's warm naked body under the green checked flannel robe. Just one pull on that loose loop she had tied around her waist...No, concentrate on breakfast. It was easier for her to stay tuned in to her body's desire for Jannika than it was to feel her heart soften and expand because of this beautiful woman. Even though she acted open and available, the truth was she hadn't allowed any woman access to the deepest part of her heart. She was amazed that the thread of connection between her and Jannika hadn't broken, even after eighteen years of life and love and heartbreak. Every time she talked to Jannika, touched her, and spent time with her, more threads seemed to wind around that initial connection, making it stronger and everlasting.

Jannika said, "I think I'll enjoy the lovely breakfast you're going to make, then stop by my place on the way to the store and take a shower and change."

"Sounds like a plan." Lee kept her hands busy whisking eggs in a bowl.

Jannika turned to go upstairs.

"Hey, Nick," Lee said.

"Hey what?"

"Thanks for staying the night." She let her happiness pour from her heart.

Jannika blushed. "You're very welcome." She flashed open the robe and ran upstairs.

❖

Jannika got to the store five minutes before opening, humming U2's "Beautiful Day." Sarah met her at the door.

"Well, someone's in a good...whoa. I know you're my boss and everything." Sarah lowered her voice, whispering, "But way to go, boss lady."

Jannika felt her cheeks flush.

"I love when people are happy," Sarah said. "It's all around you. What would you like me to do today? Let's do something fun."

"I planned on changing out the displays on the shelves above the windows, if you think that'll be fun."

"I have a feeling anything we do today will be fun. I'll get the ladder," Sarah said.

"I'll grab some books."

Sarah held on to the stepladder, and they passed books back and forth, changing out the displays. They spent the remainder of the day busy helping many of their regular customers and two busloads of tourists who were on their way to a craft festival in the White Mountains.

She called Lee after she got home. "Hey you."

"Hey yourself. I've got some lasagna in the oven and thought you might like to come over for dinner tonight. I'd also like to show you my park, maybe Sunday?" Lee asked.

Everything that had happened with Lee the past couple of days was wonderful and terrifying too. Was it all too good to be true? That she could be with her after all these years? Doubts flashed through her mind.

"Lee, I think I need a night at my place. To...I don't know. My day started out great as you know, but then it went downhill. Sunday sounds great, though." She knew that if she was alone with Lee at the farmhouse, she'd be spending the night again, which sounded wonderful to all of her body but only part of her brain. Things felt almost too easy and too comfortable with Lee. She was in unknown territory and didn't trust her footing.

"I'm disappointed that I won't be seeing you tonight, but completely understand about needing time to yourself." Jannika warmed to Lee's understanding. "When I feel overloaded, I need to get away and be by myself. I usually go to the woods."

"Am I supposed to say color me surprised? It's interesting that for both of us elements of our jobs are also what replenishes us."

"We both love our jobs. I'll pick you up late morning on Sunday. Around eleven?"

"But we might talk before then, right?"

"I hope so," Lee said. "Good night."

"Good night." She hoped a night alone would be exactly what she needed.

Chapter Nineteen

They drove south, passing two-hundred-year-old farm-houses set close to the road and clusters of new homes set down long driveways and built on old farmland. Jannika thought the new developments tried in vain to hold on to a bit of history with names like Orchard Estates, The Maples, and Birchwood Acres. The vibrant yellows and reds of the October trees were gone, only the stubborn brown oak leaves remaining on the trees. She loved fall in New England and couldn't imagine living anywhere else.

"There was frost on the pumpkin this morning, as my grandmother used to say." Lee reached over and held Jannika's hand.

"And I saw two woolly bear caterpillars this morning in my driveway. I can never remember, is it when the brown bands are large there's a bad winter coming, or is it the black bands?" She thought she sounded like a high school student. Part of her did feel like a teenager again around Lee. And now they were going to the state park. Into the woods. She felt physically charged at the prospect of being along in the woods with Lee. Again. She tried to pay attention to the conversation and not how Lee's lips formed words.

"The black bands. How did yours look?"

"I think there was a lot of black on the ends, not much brown," Jannika said. She turned her head to look at Lee and squeezed her hand. She decided to tell Lee what she was feeling instead of trying to act cool. "This might sound weird, but I feel like I'm noticing things again since we met. Small things, like the woolly bears."

Lee picked up Jannika's hand and kissed the back of it. "Not weird at all. I seem to be waking up with my batteries fully charged lately. I think it has something to do with the company I've been keeping." Lee flashed a big smile. "I can't wait to show you Watts Lake. It's a great little park. I think it's going to be a good fit for me."

Lee stopped the truck at a metal gate.

"Do you need any help?" Jannika asked. She wanted to be helpful. She wanted Lee to think she was competent.

"Sure." Lee put a hand-carved key ring in the shape of a loon in Jannika's hand and handed her a blaze-orange vest from the back seat. "Hunting season. You can unlock the gate, let me through, then lock her up again."

Jannika put on the vest, managed the gate, then hopped back in the truck. She noticed Lee watching her and felt her ears grow warm.

Lee drove down a pine needle carpeted road and pulled the truck into the *Park Manager Only* spot next to a small brown house with white trim. They hopped out of the truck. Lee put on her orange vest and Jannika handed her the loon key ring.

"Let's take a walk around, and then I'll show you the cabin and the office on the way out. You might want to grab your hat and gloves. It can feel colder in the park than out here in the parking lot."

"I don't think I ever feel cold when I'm close to you." Jannika pulled on a hat and mittens that Aunt Gunnie knit her a couple of years ago. She had a chest full of hats, mittens, sweaters, and afghans that her aunt had made her since she was a little girl.

Whenever she wanted to feel close to Aunt Gunnie, she would snuggle up with one of her multicolored crocheted afghans. She'd lost some of them when she left her mother's house, but Aunt Gunnie was a prolific knitter and crocheter.

Lee's cheeks turned pink and she offered her arm to Jannika.

They walked the roads of Watts Lake State Park while Lee told her the history of the park and identified trees and bushes along the way. Their breath made little clouds in the crisp November air. Lee pointed to one of the park's lean-tos.

"Did you ever camp in one of these?" Lee grabbed the side of the lean-to, hoisted herself up on the platform, and held out a hand, pulling Jannika up.

"No, after my last summer at camp, I went to college, then moved near Portland. I visit my mormor, my grandma, in New Sweden and sometimes see my mom in Stillmeadow up in Maine, but not camping. It always reminded me of you."

Lee wrapped her arms around Jannika and whispered in her ear, "And that was a bad thing?"

"A very bad thing, I'm afraid." She tipped her head to the side and offered her neck to Lee's warm lips. "When I was in the woods, I'd think of you. Hell, even when I wasn't in the woods, I'd think of you." Her last few words caught in her throat as Lee drew her closer, her tongue circling the small hollow behind Jannika's ear.

"I thought of you more than a few times over the years," Lee whispered, "and you taste incredible." Lee's hands slid down to the small of Jannika's back and she pulled her closer. Jannika wrapped her arms around Lee and looked into her eyes. She touched Lee's temple.

"Your eyes haven't changed at all. When I look into your eyes, it's like I'm here with you now and I'm with your younger self too." She took off her mittens behind Lee's back and stuffed them into Lee's coat pockets. She leaned into Lee's embrace.

"Your eyes are the same too," Lee said, "but I see a strength in them and in you that you hadn't developed yet back then." Lee took a step back from their embrace and held Jannika's hands in hers. "I really like when you show me that sassy side of you." She smiled. "It's nice to know it's still there. I'm so happy we met again. I probably shouldn't share this, but I have this little war going on inside of me."

"Tell me?"

"When we're apart I think about getting to know you better and wanting to learn about all those years since camp till now. I want to see where this is going. And I don't want to scare you away by saying things—like, I want you to meet my family and my friends from Maine. But I also have these other thoughts." Lee stepped closer to her again and slid her hand under the back of Jannika's jacket.

"Other thoughts?" Jannika leaned her hips forward. She didn't want to admit it to herself, but she did want to meet Lee's family, and she wanted Lee to meet Aunt Gunnie and Marcy. She didn't know she could feel this scared and excited at the same time. She wasn't sure if she liked it, so she tried to focus on her body's insistence to being closer to Lee.

"Yes." Lee laughed. "You know what thoughts I'm talking about. But I really want to know what you're thinking, about our meeting again, our dates." Lee moved her face closer to hers.

"Not with you this close to me." Her breath quickened. She was very aware of Lee's lips. She backed away just as Lee took a step back. She took her mittens out of Lee's jacket and worked them with her hands as she spoke.

"I can't believe that we met again. It feels surreal sometimes, because I spent a lot of time wondering about you, and where you were, and what you were doing. I had Leslie in my mind all those years, and bang, now here's Lee. I feel like I have a crush on you all over again. You were the smartest, kindest, and sexiest person I had ever met. Whatever has happened in your life these past years seems to have enriched all of that and you take my breath away."

"Oh, Nick." Lee took Jannika's mittens from her hands, put them back into her pockets, and took Jannika's bare hands again.

"I think I do want to meet your family and I want you to meet Aunt Gunnie and Marcy and Edgar and his wife. All my people. But that also feels pretty scary to me. I've had some rough times with my family in the past. But every time I see you, I want to spend more time with you. It feels good."

"It feels like we're supposed to be here, together," Lee said.

"Maybe we always were." Jannika's heart beat faster as she said the words, and she felt her face grow warm.

Lee brought the backs of Jannika's hands to her lips and kissed each knuckle, then turned her hands over and kissed the middle of each palm. She placed one of Jannika's hands at her waist while she drew circles with her tongue in the center of Jannika's other palm. Her eyes never left Jannika's.

"Oh my, I'm warmer out here than I thought I'd be."

"Let's see if I can warm you up even more." Lee's mouth found hers and they kissed.

Lee's lips sent a message to the rest of her body. A reminder of the last time they kissed and what followed.

Lee removed her vest and coat and helped Jannika off with hers. They fumbled with buttons and zippers while they continued to kiss and move in awkward circles inside the lean-to.

Jannika took Lee's hand and guided it to her, then past the zipper on her pants.

"Oh my, you are so wet." Lee walked Jannika backward to the lean-to wall.

"I told you—I feel warm when I'm with you."

When Jannika's back touched the wall, she unzipped Lee's pants and slid them down over her hips. Jannika's lips rested near Lee's ear and she drew the tip of her tongue along its outer edge. Her breath quickened as Lee's fingers found her clit.

"Hey you, my ass is going to get cold."

"You won't notice it," Jannika said.

"I won't?" She put a hand on the wall next to Jannika to steady herself and gave Jannika a slow kiss.

Jannika grabbed Lee's ass with one hand and urged Lee's legs apart with the other. Then she parted Lee with her thumb and one finger and lightly teased her slick inner lips with another finger.

Lee answered by sliding a finger into Jannika and kissing her again.

"Ouch!" One of Jannika's hands went to her head. The other pulled away from Lee as she steadied herself against the wall.

Lee gently removed her hand from Jannika's pants. "Did you hit your head? I'm so sorry. Let me see."

"Hey, I'm okay." Jannika's hands grabbed Lee's behind. "Come closer."

Lee took a deep breath, pulled up her pants, and zipped them. "I want you, Nick. Every inch of me wants you. And being here, being in the woods with you again, only supercharges that feeling."

"I know. Same for me."

"Let's save your head and go someplace more comfortable." Lee grabbed their jackets and vests from the floor. They tried to help each other with their jackets, but started laughing so hard they gave up.

"Got your mittens?"

"No, you have them—they're in your jacket."

"Here, put them on and come with me." Lee took Jannika's mittened hand and they power-walked back to the cottage that housed the park office. She unlocked the door and led Jannika upstairs. "Follow me."

"I always get the best view."

"Now I'm blushing." Lee flipped a switch and a gas heater sprang to life, heating the small space in a couple of minutes.

"Smells nice in here. Like bacon and wood smoke." Jannika took off her things and dropped them on the couch. Then she took off Lee's coat and unbuttoned her shirt.

"Country girl's aphrodisiac."

They laughed, then kissed. With each kiss, their tongues found new ways to make memories.

Lee unbuttoned Jannika's shirt, then traced a line down the center of her chest and belly to the button on the waist of her jeans. Then she traced a line back up again and slid Jannika's bra straps down over her shoulders slowly, one at a time.

"You're so beautiful. My amazing Nick." Lee ran the edge of her thumb along Jannika's cheek and jawline. She outlined the cups of Jannika's bra with her fingertips.

Jannika's hands caught Lee's hips. She wanted Lee. On top of her, inside her, next to her. All her mind could think of was how to get closer.

"Lee, I…"

Lee kissed her chin and took her hand. She led her to the other side of the small room and opened a door to a small bedroom. As they got closer to the bed, Jannika kissed her and they both tumbled onto the bed laughing and kissing.

❖

Jannika woke up hungry and itchy. Lee must have pulled up the wool blanket from the bottom of the bed. She smelled food cooking and threw off the blanket, found her shirt and pants, and put them on as Lee came into the little bedroom.

"You look properly tousled and sexy as hell," Jannika said.

"No one's ever told me I tousle well."

"What do I smell?" She put her arms around Lee and pulled her close.

"I found some burgers in the freezer and a can of baked beans in the cupboard. I seem to have worked up quite an appetite, and

I had a feeling you might be hungry when you woke up, oh, she who is hungry after sex."

"What time is it?"

"Around three."

"Does that mean we were…"

"Well, you weren't asleep for more than an hour and I didn't fall asleep, so yes, we were heavily involved for more than three hours."

"I prefer to call the way we spent our time *smokin' hot sex*. It sounds so much better than *heavily involved*. That sounds like a crime scene or something."

Lee shook her head. "Come with me, have some food." Lee turned and gave her a plate with a plain burger and some baked beans.

"I think we already did *that*, several times." She blew Lee a kiss. "Is there any ketchup?"

"You are adorable. Especially with your hair sticking up like that."

"What?" Jannika patted her hair, then gave up and stuck her tongue out at Lee.

"Very cute. I seem to remember that you were the girl who used all the ketchup in camp, weren't you? Ketchup on everything." Lee plated her food. "Try the fridge."

"Hooray. Ketchup and mustard and some dried-up leafy things."

Lee said, "Huh. I assumed the summer staff did a final cleanup of everything, but I should've checked. Good thing we came."

"Yes, coming was a damn good thing. We should come more often, don't you think?" Jannika felt a little punchy. Or maybe this was what joy felt like.

"Is this what sex does to you? I like it."

"I think this is what damn good, smokin' hot sex with you does to me." Jannika speared a bite of burger and rolled it in the small mound of ketchup on her plate.

"I won't tell you you're ruining that meat. I don't want to spoil your good mood." Lee looked positively pained, but her tone was teasing.

She licked her lips. "Not the first time someone's told me that. Not ruining. Making tastier." She took another bite and smiled.

Lee watched her eat. "Speaking of food, I've been wanting to ask you something and the food reminded me. I go home to my parents every November after the season is over and spend a couple of weeks around Thanksgiving visiting them, my sisters and brothers, and my assorted nieces and nephews. I was wondering if you might want to come up for Thanksgiving weekend?"

"Oh, Lee, that sounds wonderful and intimidating as hell at the same time. Don't you have something like eleven brothers and sisters?"

"No, it's not that bad. There are six of us altogether, four girls and two boys. One brother lives in Glens Falls, New York, but the rest all still live in Maine. Mom and Dad have everyone over for Thanksgiving, including a handful of friends and friends of friends. It's an open table, more or less. I picked Thanksgiving because there would be lots of distractions."

Jannika finished chewing her last bite of burger and put down her fork. "Well, the store is closed on Thanksgiving, and Aunt Gunnie and I usually spend Thanksgiving together. Sometimes my mother comes and sometimes she doesn't. But Black Friday and the weekend can be tricky, especially with the shop local push, but most people are at home shopping online or at the malls. I'll talk to Aunt Gunnie and feel her out about it. We could make the trip up together. Your parents are over near the Kezars?"

"Another place I'd love to take you. There's a campground on Kezar Lake, and one of the sites is on an island in the middle of the lake. We could have our own little island." Lee got up and stood behind Jannika, kneading her shoulders. She bent over and whispered in Jannika's ear. Her fingers found the vee where Jannika's shirt buttoned and the soft skin below. "I hope Aunt Gunnie says yes. We have plenty of room for both of you to stay over, and if you play your cards right, I might sneak into your room in the middle of the night."

CHAPTER TWENTY

Jannika pulled up to Aunt Gunnie's house and saw her standing there, next to her 2014 Impala, clutching a large gray pocketbook. Aunt Gunnie liked to change out her vehicles every two or three years. It was her only extravagance. She'd keep a pair of shoes for ten years, her pots and pans were wedding presents from the 1970s, and she refused to trade out her old television for a flat screen. These quirks made Jannika love her aunt even more.

"We're taking the Impala. My bag's already in the back—we're all set. Your car doesn't need extra miles and mine could use a few. Pass me your bag and we'll hit the road." Aunt Gunnie held out a hand for Jannika's bag.

"Auntie, I can put my bag in your car. And thanks, it'll be nice to drive a fancy-schmancy car. And double thanks for doing this."

Aunt Gunnie pressed the car key into Jannika's hand and got in the passenger's side. "From what you tell me, she seems like a nice sort. Let's see what the family is like."

Jannika found Aunt Gunnie's favorite oldies radio station and they sang along like they had done for as long as Jannika could remember. No one on her mother's side of the family used any more words than they had to. Aunt Gunnie always explained, "We're Swedish, we don't talk, we do." But Jannika loved that her aunt was different from the rest of her family. It was one of the things that made her feel close to her. During a span of what seemed like unending commercials, Jannika turned the radio's volume down.

"I like this person a lot. I think it's important that you know that."

"I didn't think we'd be coming all this way if you didn't."

"I mean, she does something to my heart." Jannika put her right hand on her chest.

Aunt Gunnie said softly, "That other girl, after you broke up...you weren't well. I want you to have someone, like I did with your Uncle Charlie."

"I think she could be my Uncle Charlie." Jannika barely whispered the words.

"Time will tell." Aunt Gunnie patted her leg and turned up the volume on the radio. "You need to take the next left if you're going to Rumford." The Brothers Four were harmonizing about their roof having a hole in it. It felt like when she was in grade school and Auntie would drive up to get her for a long weekend. Jannika learned a lot of songs from the sixties on those drives. They sang their way to Lee's family's farm.

The first thing Jannika noticed was that Lee's farmhouse property in New Hampshire looked like a miniature version of the Thompson farm. No wonder she looked so at home there, Jannika thought, taking in the barn on the right and the white farmhouse on the left. But this farmhouse looked like it had been added on to several times over. She spotted three porches, two ells, and some kind of archway that looked like it joined a small cottage to one of the ells.

Her stomach was knotted. She got out of the car and grabbed their bags. "Which door do you think we should use?" She thought about offering to take her aunt's bag, but knew better.

Aunt Gunnie came around to the driver's side of the car. "You're jumpy as a cat. Take a good breath of this air and let's wait a minute. With all these vehicles somebody's sure to come out."

Less than a minute later, a tall slender man wearing a buffalo plaid wool shirt came out the side door. "Hi, can you help me? I've got to find the diaper bag and something called a pack-it-up for my cousin?" He opened the back of a Subaru Forester.

Aunt Gunnie met the man at the car. "It's a Pack 'n Play. I didn't know they still made those. There it is." She pointed to the folded up item in question in the rear of the car. "Maybe you can help us out too. Should we go in there?" She indicated the side door.

"Only if you want to be in the middle of a tornado. That's the kitchen, and my aunt Peggy's domain. I ran through. Follow me, we'll go in the front. I'm Jason."

"I'm Jannika and this is my Aunt Gunnie. We're friends of—"

"Lee, I know. C'mon in and give me a minute to pass off this stuff, and I'll find her."

They dragged their bags across the gravel driveway, up the porch, and into the house. The smell of roasting turkey, apples and cinnamon, and sausage greeted them along with the voices of children playing.

Jason and the baby gear disappeared into a room on their left. Aunt Gunnie looked up and down the short hallway.

"It was a long drive," Aunt Gunnie said.

"Oh, I'm sorry. There must be a bathroom someplace." Jannika backed up and poked her head in a small doorway. "Here, Auntie."

While her aunt was in the bathroom, Jannika watched children of varying sizes, shapes, and colors play in the sunroom off the hallway. She heard louder adult voices down the other end of the hall. Aunt Gunnie stepped out of the bathroom and closed the door behind her, just as a woman came walking down the hall toward them, with a welcoming smile.

"Jannika. And you must be Jannika's aunt. Lee told me to look out for you both. I'm Bonnie, but everyone in the family calls me Bon-Bon, use whichever you want. Let me take your bags to the cottage. It's very sweet, you'll love it. Did you see my kids out front? Well, if they weren't there, they're around here somewhere. And in there"—she pointed to an arched entry at the end of the dining room—"you'll find who you're looking for." Bonnie stuck out an elbow and nudged Jannika twice.

Aunt Gunnie led the way through the dining room toward the large family room. "You never did like a commotion," she said to Jannika.

Jannika looked into a room of faces and her heart skipped a beat or two. Maybe she shouldn't have come. This was Lee's family. Having her fantasies play out in real life was one thing. But Lee's family was reality. Lee didn't exist in a vacuum. She turned to face Aunt Gunnie, to tell her maybe this wasn't such a good idea after all, and felt a strong hand on the small of her back.

"I'm so happy you're here," Lee said. She took Jannika's hand. "Thank you so much for coming, Aunt Gunnie. It's so nice to meet you." She held out her other hand.

Aunt Gunnie shook Lee's hand. "Thank you for inviting us."

A woman who looked like a shorter, fuller version of Lee came into the family room and made a straight line to them.

"Mom, this is Jannika and her Aunt Gunnie."

"I'm Peggy and Lee's dad Wally is over there with the bundle of dogs and kids. I'm so glad you could make the drive up. We're twenty-five this year, twenty-nine if you count the dogs." Peggy laughed. "Are you hungry? Help yourselves to some snacks on the sideboard over there. We'll start bringing out the feast in a few minutes."

"Do you need any help, Mom?" Lee asked.

"We'd be happy to help," Aunt Gunnie said.

"I certainly don't need you banging and bumping around the kitchen any more than you've done all morning, waiting for *someone* to get here." Peggy waved her daughter away and hooked her arm around Gunnie's. "But I'll take you up on your offer, Gunnie. Those two are in their own little world."

"Oh, Mom," Lee said.

"You two can gather everybody up, and mix them up at tables. I don't want all adults in one room and kids in the other like last year."

"Yes, ma'am," Lee said. She waited until her mother and Gunnie had turned the corner. "Come see the side porch."

"The side porch?" Jannika two stepped behind Lee who was holding her hand and headed for the front door.

"Yes." Lee shut the front door behind them. "We have a front porch." She led Jannika around the corner of the house. "And a side porch." She spun around and backed Jannika against the side of the house and kissed her.

Jannika dipped as her knees went weak and Lee pressed against her.

"I missed you."

"I missed you too. Your family is—"

"One more." Lee's hungry lips met Jannika's.

Their kiss was slow and deep and said all the words Jannika couldn't yet say out loud.

Lee stepped back and looked into Jannika's eyes. Jannika returned her gaze with a heart full of desire and happiness.

Lee smiled and took her hand again. "Let's go get 'em."

They went room to room, letting everyone know that it was time to eat. When they found Lee's father, he took two toddlers off his lap and smiled.

"Nice to meet you, Mr. Thompson." Jannika extended her hand.

"That's Wally." He shook her hand and tipped his head toward Lee. "You're even prettier than Lee said."

Jannika's face burned. "Thank you."

"My parents have both made me feel exactly fourteen years old in a matter of minutes," Lee said.

"Well, you are very pretty. You run a bookstore, my daughter tells me."

"Dad can we talk and walk? Mom's waiting for us."

"Yes, we can talk over dinner. You're sitting at our table."

A man Lee identified as her brother Brian appeared at the end of the hall. "C'mon, slowpokes."

"Is Brian your older brother or younger brother?" Jannika asked as they made their way to the dining room.

"Don't bother trying to keep track of them yet—you'll figure them out after a while." Lee put one hand on the small of Jannika's back as they walked down the hall.

The familiar clench of anxiety gripped Jannika's stomach and she looked around the room for Aunt Gunnie, who finally emerged from the kitchen and put a huge green bean casserole on the table. Jannika's stomach relaxed as she took her seat.

"I'm next to you," Aunt Gunnie said and took Jannika's hand under the table.

Jannika looked around the room. This was her dream Thanksgiving. A huge room—no, two rooms—of family and friends, in a big old farmhouse, people laughing and joking, babies fussing, and an occasional dog passing by for a pat or scratch behind an ear. She looked across the table at Peggy and imagined herself looking across a table at a much older Lee. She was afraid of being happy. No, she thought, she was afraid of having it all and losing it all someday. She might lose the store in the near future. She still hadn't called Joe to find out what, if anything was going on. She didn't know how she could start planning a life with Lee if she might not have the store, or be able to stay in the area. She squeezed Aunt Gunnie's hand for reassurance as she looked down at her plate.

"Can I pour you some water? Or something else?" Peggy had a large white pitcher in her hand and was pouring glasses of water.

"Water's fine, thank you." Jannika looked at Peggy once again and then at Lee. She felt her heart expand. It had been difficult this past week to think of anything but Lee and her together. Kissing Lee, wrapping her arms around Lee, laughing with Lee, and making love with Lee. But she felt something else now, and she allowed herself to feel it. When she looked into Lee's eyes, when she was with Lee, she felt like she had come home.

"I think we're still missing a couple of people, but let's say grace and get on with it," Wally said. "I'm starving. Who else is starving?" he yelled into the other room.

Lee took Jannika's hand under the table.

"We are thankful for the food on this table and the people surrounding the table. We are thankful for all the hands who helped put the food on this table and who have helped the people who surround this table. Now let's eat!"

Jannika watched as everyone sprang into action, passing dishes around and across the table, taking dishes into the other room, and bringing back more stuffing and sweet potatoes with cranberries, green bean casserole, and a pasta and broccoli dish. This was very different from the quiet Thanksgivings she would have with Aunt Gunnie and Uncle Charlie and her mother. She found it hard to follow all the conversations happening at once. She felt Lee squeeze her knee.

"Too much?" Lee said, softly enough for only Jannika to hear.

"No, I'm okay." Jannika smiled.

"Jannika, how big is your bookstore?" Peggy asked.

"About the size of the small bookstore we passed in the village on the way here. Just the right size for Grangeton."

"Do you have those Louise Penny books? I love those." Peggy asked.

"Oh, the Chief Inspector Gamache ones?" Bonnie added.

"Inspector who?" One of Lee's brothers passed a gravy boat across the table to Jannika.

"Are you talking about Rich's house inspection?" came a voice from the other room.

"Beats my head flat," said Wally.

Jannika burst out laughing.

"There's a man can turn a phrase," said Aunt Gunnie.

"And then some, Gunnie." Peggy laughed along with most everyone at their end of the table.

Chapter Twenty-one

Lee felt happiness settle into her bones. She felt like she'd stepped through a gray curtain that had muted the world since Shannon's death. She didn't know if it would last five minutes or fifty years, but she knew in that moment, for the first time in five years, there was another side to that gray curtain. She loved hearing Jannika laugh with her family.

"I'm going to refill this pitcher of water. Anyone need anything from the kitchen?" Lee asked.

A chorus of *no thank you*s and one *more butter* answered her.

"I'll go with you." Aunt Gunnie got up from her seat and followed Lee into the back kitchen.

Lee turned on the tap and waited for the water to run cold.

"Can that wait a minute?" asked Aunt Gunnie.

"Sure, is everything okay?" Lee shut off the water and set the pitcher in the sink. She hoped she hadn't done anything to offend Jannika's aunt. She could sense an important conversation was about to happen. Her throat felt tight, but she knew she would answer Aunt Gunnie honestly, no matter what she asked her.

"I don't beat around the bush. I like you. You're the girl she met at camp that summer, aren't you?"

"Yes, ma'am. I am."

"No ma'ams. I'm Aunt Gunnie to Nick and to you too."

"Okay." Lee felt honored that Jannika wanted to bring the person who meant the most to her up to her family Thanksgiving.

"You helped my Nick a lot that summer. She's not had an easy go of it. I won't go into her business, but let's leave it at that. She doesn't need any fly-by-night romance right now. I don't think that's what you're up to, but I'm just looking out for her. She's a good girl with a big heart."

"I can tell that. I've lived enough of my life to know when something is just a romance and when it is something much more than that. I care deeply for your niece, Aunt Gunnie. That's why I wanted you both to come up here. I want you both to feel like you're part of this family. If you're asking my intentions, they are serious. I wouldn't want to do anything ever to hurt her."

"You look good together, you two. My niece might be a little skittish at times. Don't let that get in the way. You hear?"

"I hear you."

"I'm going back. You better get that water before people go all parched on you." Aunt Gunnie left the kitchen just as her mom was entering.

"Are you okay, Gunnie? Everything okay?"

"Yep, just getting back to the table." Gunnie walked down the hallway to the dining room.

"Everything's okay, Mom. Aunt Gunnie and I were just having a chat."

Her mother looked from her daughter to the hallway and back again.

"Really, Mom. But Jannika is probably wondering."

Her mother nodded. "She was putting on a good face, but I think she's concerned."

"Can you get the water? I've got to get back out there," Lee said as she left the room.

Jannika looked relieved when Lee sat back down beside her.

"Is everything okay?" she mouthed to Lee.

"Almost time for the game," a voice shouted from the other room. Then the sound of chairs scraping the floor and dishes being stacked carried into the dining room. Their group took the hint and started moving things off the table.

Lee nodded and smiled. She wanted every Thanksgiving to be like this from now on, with Jannika beside her.

❖

While Lee was in the kitchen with Gunnie, Jannika started to have a difficult time making conversation. Without Aunt Gunnie and Lee beside her, she felt like what she was, an outsider. She felt foolish thinking that maybe all of this could be hers, when she knew it was just a dream, like the happy family dreams she'd had growing up. But she didn't grow up like Lee did, in this wonderful whole family where everyone loved and supported each other. She didn't know how to be one of these people. She'd had a broken childhood.

Even now, with Lee back beside her, her doubts overwhelmed her. Lee wouldn't be able to build a life with someone who wasn't whole. She'd leave eventually.

Now listening to Lee's family and watching them have fun and kid around with each other stung. It was everything she wanted but couldn't have. She needed to talk to Lee. Alone.

"Can we go somewhere and talk?" Jannika put her napkin on the table.

"Sure, let's grab some stuff and bring it into the kitchen first." Lee passed the almost empty dish of sweet potatoes to Jannika and took some dinner plates from the table.

After they put their dishes in the kitchen, Lee led Jannika out to the porch.

"Is this okay?"

"Is there someplace more private?" Jannika couldn't stop the strain from leaking into her voice.

"Are you okay? What's wrong?"

"I just need to talk for a minute. I think I need to take a break." Jannika's stomach churned and she swallowed hard. Her hands started to sweat. She rubbed them on her pants.

"Are you not feeling well? I hope it wasn't Bon-Bon's broccoli thing—I told her she shouldn't make that, it was just a weird combination to begin with."

"Lee..."

"Sorry, I'm in a bit of a panic here, and I'm trying not to be."

"It's not you." Jannika looked past Lee to the barn.

"Oh God, not that. If you start with that, there's no place for me to go. Nothing I can do. What's wrong? Did I bring you here too soon? We can slow down. Do you want to slow down?" Lee reached for Jannika.

"No, please don't touch me. It'll just make it more difficult."

"I don't think I want to make this easy for you." Lee ran her fingers through her hair.

Jannika looked at Lee.

"You are wonderful. You're beautiful and sexy and smart and everything I always wanted. But I looked at your family and everything, and I don't know how to do this. I don't know how to have a relationship with you. I don't know how to do the perfect family thing. It's me. It's how I am, I guess. But it's not you. It's not even us, just the two of us. You're perfect. Your family is wonderful. They are everything anyone could dream of in a family. They're everything I ever dreamed of in a family, but I let go of those dreams a long time ago, and I need time. I need a break, to step back and figure things out." She felt sick to her stomach. The hurt and confusion on Lee's face made her want to wrap her arms around her. "To be totally sure I'm here in the now and not trying to capture a long-ago dream."

"How long a break? Will you still spend the night?" Lee shifted from one foot to another. She put her hands in her front jeans pockets.

Jannika saw Lee's eyes fill and felt her own tears threaten.

"I can't stay. I'm sorry. Let me go talk to my auntie and apologize to your family." She shook her head and her tears overflowed onto her cheeks. She wiped her face with the back of her hands. "I need to think about things. About me. I need to figure some things out about myself."

Lee reached up and gently ran her fingers over Jannika's forehead and down the sides of her face. "This was too soon, wasn't it. Whatever you need. You go talk to your aunt and I'll talk to my family. Then you can say good-bye to them. Most of them won't notice. They're watching the game." She smiled a crooked smile.

Lee's touch took her breath away. "Thanks. I'll go find Auntie." Jannika followed Lee into the house. She found her aunt in the kitchen with Peggy.

"Auntie, can I borrow you for a minute?"

"Well, I don't want to leave Peggy with all this." Her aunt spread her arms wide.

"Gunnie, I have a dishwasher and several other sets of hands that can help. You've done so much already. Why don't you take some pie and go in the other room with the girls."

"I'll stay here and help, Mom," Lee said.

Gunnie and Peggy stopped what they were doing and looked at each other, and then Gunnie followed Jannika out of the kitchen and down the hallway to the empty sun porch.

"I'm so sorry, Auntie, but I need to leave."

"Don't you feel okay?" Aunt Gunnie reached up to touch Jannika's forehead.

"Lee and I just had a talk. I decided I need a break from our relationship. Please don't say anything right now. I really need to get out of here."

"Did Lee do something?"

"No, it's not Lee. It's me. Lee is wonderful. Probably the most wonderful person on the planet. Auntie...please?"

"We need to apologize to these good folks. I can tell you, Jannika, I'll do most anything for you, but this doesn't sit right with me. It feels downright rude and ungrateful."

"I was thinking we'd say you weren't feeling well." She gave her aunt a hopeful look.

"No, you're the one who is feeling bad. You tell them that. I can see there's something eating at you. I've known you all your life. This big family too much for you? Is that it?"

She saw the concern in her aunt's face. "I promise, we'll talk. I don't even totally understand myself."

They went back in the house and found Lee and Peggy still in the kitchen. Jannika apologized to Peggy and went to find Wally and apologized to him as well.

"Maybe you should stay here and rest until you feel better," Wally said with one eye on the television.

"She'll probably feel better in her own bed, Dad." Lee looked at her. "I'll get your bags while you and Aunt Gunnie say good-bye, and I'll meet you out there."

They went from room to room. Jannika felt like she was saying good-bye to more than just the people in this farmhouse. Her legs shook as she and Aunt Gunnie walked down the stairs to the driveway.

"The bags are in the car," Lee said. "Please give me a call and let me know how you are both doing."

Jannika got Aunt Gunnie settled into the passenger seat and went around to the driver's side. A cauldron of emotions boiled in her throat and she couldn't speak. Lee stepped closer and attempted to pull her into an embrace.

Jannika backed away and opened the car door. "I've got to go." The words caught in her throat. Part of her wanted to fold herself into Lee's arms.

"Please drive safe. Promise me," Lee said.

Jannika got in the car. "I promise." She shut the door and rolled down the window.

"I understand that you think you need time to yourself, but I don't understand the big change. I went into the kitchen to get water and when I came out, everything changed. I hope you'll explain that to me sometime."

"I need to go now," Jannika said.

Aunt Gunnie sat beside her in silence.

"Okay. But we'll talk soon, right?"

"I'll call you." She started the car, rolled the window up, and drove away. She tried not to look in the rearview mirror, but did anyway and saw her beautiful Lee, her family's farm behind her and the sun setting behind the tall pines.

❖

Lee backed away from the car and right into one of the small maple trees that lined the upper driveway. She hung onto the tree and watched Jannika's car until it rounded the curve in the driveway. Every part of her wanted to be with Jannika right now and help her sort out what was going on inside her. She wanted to hold her, let her vent, make her food, whatever she needed. This wasn't how the day was supposed to end. She'd wanted to give Jannika this perfect day with her family. She'd wanted her to feel at home and welcome. Not this...whatever this was.

She walked to the gazebo on the back side of the main house. It was her favorite place to sit and think at night. When she was younger, she would sit on the floor, so no one from the main house could see her, but she could see the sky and the small lights coming from the houses down in the valley. Today she sat on one of the benches and just stared out.

Lee heard someone walking toward the gazebo, but she didn't look up.

"Hey, sis. If you want to be alone, tell me, but I thought you might want company."

"Hey, Bon-Bon. Not the way I thought this day was going to go."

"She wasn't sick, was she." Bonnie sat on the bench next to Lee.

"Something about today scared her. She said she needs time to herself, that it's not me, it's her. She's afraid our family is too good for her, that what's happening with us is too good for her. Sounds to me like good-bye. Damn it, Bon, she's…she's…"

Bonnie put her arm around her shoulders. "What? She's what, sweetie?"

"I love her. And that love broke through all the stuff I've built up after Shannon—it burst right through. The night I first saw her again, what were the chances of that? Of meeting her again after all these years? But what were the chances of someone killing my wife? Why bother loving someone? I feel like such a fool. One minute you think you have a life, a future with someone, and then it's taken from you." Tears ran down her face.

"No one plans to have someone taken from them like Shannon was taken from you, and no one plans for love to come along and grab you by the heart. You know that life can be painful, no one has to remind you of that, but I think you might need a reminder right now that life can be full of joy and love and hope. When you told me you met up with that girl from camp, the one you told me about all those years ago, I thought how unbelievable and wonderful that was. That was a gift you were both given. You can't just ignore that or toss it away. I saw how she looked at you, how you looked at each other. You two are nuts for each other. All of us could see it."

"But it's not only up to me. What am I supposed to do, just wait?" Lee sniffed.

"I think you need to be gentle and patient with her right now. Like you said, something scared her. But if you give up on your relationship, and she hears that or sees that, you'll have no chance at all. You need to hold the love and the hope for both of you right now. I know you can do that. If that's what you want, I know you can." Bonnie squeezed her shoulders.

Hope. Could she? For now, that was all she had.

Chapter Twenty-two

The car was silent as they left Rumford and headed west. As they drove through Bethel, Gunnie put a hand on Jannika's shoulder.

"You need to eat and I could go for a snack. I saw how much food was on your plate at Lee's. I think there's a Chinese place somewhere here." Gunnie leaned forward as she searched the storefronts. "There, on the right, see it?"

Jannika pulled into the parking lot. She leaned her head back and closed her eyes. "I'm really not hungry. What do you want, Auntie?"

"Honey, right now I want to go back in time and stop you from leaving Lee's Thanksgiving. But I can't. All we can do is go forward. I don't know how, right yet, but I know you're upset and tired. Not a good combination for driving. Let's eat, find a place to sleep tonight, and talk. Then be on the road bright and early."

Jannika's voice was as flat as the bottom of a pan. "What do you want to eat?"

"Chicken lo mein." Gunnie looked out the passenger window. "Large, and some of that fried rice. And please get some extra napkins and forks."

Jannika was in and out in fifteen minutes.

"I talked to a nice young man while you were in there, and I've found a place to stay up the road. We can eat and talk and get some rest. I don't think we should be on the road after dark." Gunnie looked over at Jannika.

"Fine, Auntie, show me how to get there."

They checked in to the motel and got settled in the room. Once Aunt Gunnie started eating, she noticed her stomach felt empty too. They ate their Chinese food from the boxes in silence, passing the cartons back and forth across the tiny table.

Aunt Gunnie broke the silence with, "I'm so sorry about whatever has got you all balled up. Do you want to talk to me about what happened at Lee's?"

"You saw her family. They were like a TV movie. I can't be part of that. I don't know how to be a part of that life." Jannika walked over to one of the beds and sat on the edge.

"She's got a friendly family. They all seem nice. But they're people, honey, just like the rest of us. They have their troubles and their hurts too."

"I never told you, but when Mama and I had our last big fight, when I left home, she told me that my father left because of me. That he wanted just her, and I was baggage."

"Your mama has said a lot of downright mean things to people she loves. I don't think she knows how to do anything else. She was hurt when your father left, but she fed that hurt every day of her life and of yours. She wouldn't let it heal—she just picked and picked at that scab every single day. That's not living a life. Some people spend a lot of time picking at scabs and making them bleed again. They can't seem to get on with their own life." Aunt Gunnie got up and sat down next to Jannika on the bed. "You never seemed to be the sort who wanted to keep picking at those scabs."

"I did make a plan while I was at community college to leave and get away from her and the awful fighting," Jannika said.

"Yes, you did. You got great grades, lined up that job, and applied to that school over in Portland. You did that all yourself. You worked at those bookstores and made a life, and then you came down here and you're making a life here." Aunt Gunnie patted her thigh.

"Well, you and Uncle Charlie helped me with the paperwork for school, but you're right—I did all of that. But this is big, Auntie."

"I can tell, honey." Aunt Gunnie got up and grabbed two bottles of water from the take-out bag. She handed one to Jannika. "The lo mein always makes me thirsty."

Jannika opened the bottle and took a long drink. "Thanks."

"I saw the way you two are together. It made me happy to see you like that."

"I don't know if I can do this." Jannika's voice dropped.

"It's your choice and nobody else's. When that man left you and your mama, well, that's part of your story, but it's not your whole story. This isn't about your mother or your father or even me and the choices we made in our lives. This is about you. You've been working on your life since you left your mama's house. When you wanted something, you worked hard to make it happen. When things didn't work out the way you wanted, you took care of it and found another way. I'm so proud of you."

Tears filled Jannika's eyes. She knew her aunt loved her dearly, but she didn't know how closely she'd followed Jannika's life and what she thought about it, until now. She put her arms around her aunt and hugged her. Her aunt patted her back, the same way she'd done as far back as Jannika could remember.

"Let's shut those blinds. It's getting dark out, and I don't want all those people looking in here."

She knew this was Aunt Gunnie's way of ending their hug. She was probably the most touchy of all her relatives, but hugs had a time limit.

"Sure thing." Jannika got up and closed the blinds and paced the floor in front of the beds. "I don't know what to do," she said.

"Yes, you do. I know you have feelings for this girl."

"Yes, I do."

"Are you going to pick scabs from the past and let that pain blind you to what's right in front of you?"

"Whoa, Auntie."

"I'm very serious."

"I know you are," Jannika said.

"Because I love you so much."

"I love you too, Auntie. Sometimes I do let that pain get in my way."

"Are you happy with Lee?" Aunt Gunnie asked.

She knew the answer to this question. "So happy. It seems so easy to be with her. Everything falls into place when we're together."

"If happiness is plopped into your life, what do you think you should do with it?"

Jannika looked away for a moment. She pictured her life with Lee and what that might look like. Then she pictured her life without Lee and what that looked like.

"Auntie, you're right. This is no one's choice but mine. But I need to take care of something that's hanging over my head first. I haven't called Joe yet about the store."

"Why for heaven's sake not?"

"I didn't want to find out if the rumors were true. I know, don't even say it. I'm going to call him first thing when I get back to the store tomorrow."

Jannika's phone vibrated on the nightstand. She picked it up. It was a text from Lee. *You in for the night?*

Jannika's thumbs worked the phone. *We're at a motel in Bethel. We'll go home in the morning. Thanks for checking in.*

Lee texted back: *I'm going home tomorrow and am available if you need or want anything.*

Thanks. I know. I'll call you.

Chapter Twenty-three

It was Black Friday and Jannika was only about ten minutes late opening the store. No one was waiting. Her emotions were a ball of tangled spaghetti, one strand wound around another and another. A mess. There was a note on the desk from Sarah. *Please call the boss on his cellphone. He needs to talk with you. Very agitated energy.*

She didn't have time to call Joe Bosworth. Three customers came in the store. A short pudgy woman carrying a huge flowered tote bag sat down on the wooden chair next to Jannika's desk and let out a long whistle.

"I've come from Connecticut," she said.

"Oh, that's a long drive," Jannika replied. "How can I help you?"

"I read an article in the paper about how you can match people with books. Can you?" The woman fiddled with the handles of her tote bag and glanced around the store, but didn't look at Jannika.

"I like to help people find books they're looking for." Jannika turned toward the back counter and flicked the stereo system on.

"Excuse me, *helllooo*," the pudgy woman said. "All you types are the same. Airheads. Can you help me or what?"

"Can you come with me?" Jannika always led customers into an aisle where they could have a bit more privacy. Sometimes people would confess very interesting reasons for needing a particular book.

"Yeah, I guess so, whatever." The woman and her tote bag followed Jannika down an aisle.

"Now, what can I help you with?" Jannika steadied herself and put one hand on a bookshelf. Her legs were rubber. She dreaded the phone call she needed to make to Joe Bosworth. She didn't feel like helping this woman or anyone today.

"My life is...the same. Every day. Every week. Every month. The same. I don't want it to be, but it is. I don't know how to change that." The woman spoke softly and finally looked up at Jannika. Her eyes weren't the blank eyes of someone who was giving up hope. This woman's eyes had fire behind them. Jannika continued to look into the woman's face. Titles and phrases from books scrolled through Jannika's mind. One title stood out. It was a risky one, but Jannika's bookish intuition told her to go for it.

"Hmm, I know the book I want to show you. Let me see if we still have a copy." She ran her finger along the spines of the books as she walked down the rest of the aisle, around the corner, and up the next aisle. Then her finger stopped on a title. *The Diving Bell and the Butterfly* by Jean-Dominique Bauby.

"Here it is." Jannika pulled the book off the shelf, gave it a little pat, and handed it to the woman who was right behind her.

"You must know every book in this store. I probably won't like the book though. Let me see." She reached out and grabbed the book from Jannika. Then she trudged over to one of the comfy chairs, sat down, and fished inside her bag. She took out a pair of reading glasses and opened the book to read the flyleaf. Then she flipped to the back flyleaf. Then she turned the book over and read the back cover. Then she looked up at Jannika.

"I don't know. Can I start it here and if I don't like it, can you find me another one?"

"Of course you can. There's coffee up front—make yourself at home."

Jannika was rescued by a voice that called out from the front of the store, "Can someone check us out?"

"I think we need to come back again," a second voice said with a laugh, as Jannika made her way back to the front desk. A couple of college kids stood there, their arms filled with books.

Their laughter broke through Jannika's shell of irritation and she laughed with them. Even on a bad day, this was all she ever wanted to do. She rang them up and put their books into a cardboard box. "Thanks."

She felt the buzz of her phone in her pocket. She pulled it out to see a text from Lee.

A short woman with curly red hair and a camera over her shoulder came into the store and headed right for Jannika.

Am OK. Busy at store. Will call later. She returned Lee's text with flying fingers.

"Hi," the woman with the camera said, extending her hand. "Maggie Lyons from the *Grangeton Times*, and we were going to use you for this week's person of the week?"

"Oh, hi. Sorry, I forgot you were coming. Do you mind working around customers?" Jannika took a deep breath and breathed in her store, the books, the stories. She closed her eyes.

"Um, Ms. Peterson? Did I come at a bad time?"

Jannika's eyes flew open.

"No, no, sorry about that. I had a wild morning, and it might sound silly, but I was reconnecting with the store."

"That's exactly the kind of thing I'm looking for." Maggie retrieved a small tablet from her coat pocket and began thumb-typing.

"I'm honored to be the person of the week. I love reading that column every week. It's helped me get to know people here in town."

"I already have some background information that I got online, so I wanted to ask a few questions. Is it okay if I record this?" she said, tapping and swiping the screen of her tablet.

"Okay." Jannika rubbed the back of her neck. She stood up and went to the end of an aisle. An interview was the very last thing she wanted to do this morning.

"You've been in town for over a year now, and I know the *Concord Monitor* did a short piece on you a few months ago, but I'm sure a lot of folks here didn't see it. People want to know more about you." The reporter asked Jannika the usual background questions about where she grew up, what brought her to town, and what she liked about working in Grangeton. Usually Jannika could rattle off the answers to those questions, but this morning each question brought up several other questions in Jannika's mind about her future and what it might hold. Jannika answered with her mind spinning off in other directions.

Then the reporter said, "So, people say that you have a special way of matching up books with people. A couple of people in town I spoke with said they came in just to browse and you chatted with them, then put a book in their hands, and it was perfect for them. I won't mention any names in the article, but one woman said the book you gave her helped her make the decision to go back to school. Another person said they reconnected with a sister they hadn't spoken with for years after reading a book you gave them. And I've got at least ten more stories. The Pageturner has been here for eight years and it was just a used book store until you came to town. What would you call what you do?"

Jannika laughed. She didn't think *I'm really good at my job* was the answer Maggie wanted to hear. Even though it was true. "I don't think there's a name for what I do. Some people have called me a bibliotherapist, but I have no special training. A friend of mine told me I have a bookish intuition when it comes to my customers. Maybe call it *enhanced reader's advisory*?"

"What's a bibilo...?"

"Bibliotherapist? That's someone who's trained to prescribe books. If you're facing a career path choice or have had a recent life change like a divorce or giving birth, the bibliotherapist would recommend several books that might help you gain insight. But I'm not a bibiliotherapist. When I was a little girl, I spent a lot of time at the library. The books were more than stories to me—they were my friends. My aunt, Gunnie Johnson, who lives here in town, was the first person to notice that I loved to recommend books to my friends. She'd bring me to the library when she came to visit, and she and the librarian noticed me giving other kids books. They called me the junior librarian, and I loved that."

"Does your intuition serve you well in other areas of your life?"

"I wish it did. But it seems to be only with books," Jannika replied. "Excuse me."

A couple of customers had entered the store as they were talking. One was a regular, and he beelined to the sci-fi bookcase on the far wall. The other was a new customer who'd wandered around and was now walking toward Jannika's big desk at the front of the store.

"Can I help you?" Jannika asked.

"I...haven't been able to read for a while, and I want something that I don't have to think about and maybe something, I don't know, about recovery or grief or...I don't know."

The woman was in her late fifties early sixties, Jannika guessed, about her mother's age or so. She felt the reporter watching her as she motioned for the woman to follow her down the aisle of books.

"I used to read a lot," the woman said. "That was before Sally died. We were very close. I just can't seem to follow the story in any of the books I usually read. A friend said you might understand. Sally and I...lived together."

Jannika's heart softened as she looked at the woman. "That's very common after such a big loss. But you want to read?"

"Yes, if I can follow the story. It's a comfort for me."

"Hmm, I am pretty sure I have something for you. Have you ever read this series?" She pulled a book from the shelf. "They're set in a small town. It's very light, no surprises."

"Oh, you know what?" The woman's face brightened a bit. "I read the first two of these a long time ago and forgot the name of the author. I forgot all about them. Yes, these look perfect."

"I think we have the whole series there, maybe some duplicates too. I'll be right back—I have an idea for another book," Jannika said.

She walked to the front of the store and the large low bookcase in back of her desk. Her eyes scanned titles and she reached in for the slim volume. When she got up and turned around the woman was at the desk with three of the series titles. Jannika handed the woman the little book.

Jannika lowered her voice so the reporter wouldn't hear. "This is one of the best books I've read about living after losing someone—*Another Path*. Gladys Taber, the author, lived in New England. It's pretty old, but it's a great book about living after any kind of loss."

Jannika passed the little book across the desk and the woman's shoulders relaxed a little and her face softened. She whispered a thank you to Jannika and put the books on the desk. The reporter was sitting in a chair by the coffee counter, fingers flying as she typed on her tablet. Jannika wished she would go away. She finished with that customer as a smiling couple came arm in arm into the store.

"Jannika?" the man said.

"Hi, there," Jannika said and waved.

"You probably don't remember me. I was in town on business about eight months ago and stopped in for something to read."

"I hope it was a good read," Jannika said, smiling. She didn't remember him at all.

"You gave me three books with very stern instructions to read all three. Not two, but three." He smiled.

"I do remember now." Jannika nodded her head. "How are things?"

"I...*we* came by to invite you to our wedding." The man's grin looked like it might jump right off his face. "After I read those books, I knew exactly what I had to do. Those stories gave me the courage to ask this wonderful woman to marry me. And she said yes."

"I am so happy for you." Jannika shook the man's hand and the woman's hand and congratulated them. She was genuinely happy but felt self-conscious with the reporter in the store.

"We made a special trip up so I could show Lily the store and introduce you, and we want to send you an invitation. We hope you'll come."

"Thanks so much." Jannika used to be uncomfortable when people thanked her after they read a book she recommended. Especially if they brought her in a little gift or wrote her a card. When she was younger she'd thought she was the only person that books and stories mattered to so deeply. They'd helped her through her childhood, job losses, disagreements with friends, and heartbreak. Books had inspired her, healed her, and given her the courage to try new things. She'd learned to accept the small gifts and notes of thanks with gratitude and the knowledge that books mattered profoundly to other people too.

"We're going to poke around. I don't need any recommendations today," the man said. He took his fiancée's hand and led her down an aisle.

"Is this what it's like in here every day?" Maggie the reporter asked.

"Usually. Sometimes it's a little busier and sometimes a little slower, but yeah, this is what it's like," Jannika said.

"I think I got plenty here for the piece. But I don't have a photo. Do you suppose the happy couple might want their picture taken with you? I'd send them a copy."

"They might like that—I'll go ask them," Jannika said.

They were eager to have their picture taken with Jannika and wanted to talk with the reporter. All three left together, chatting.

Finally, there were just a couple of customers still in the store, two of them reading and one browsing. She picked up the store phone and dialed Joe Bosworth's number. She expected it to go direct to voicemail as usual, but he picked up on the fifth ring.

"Hi, sunshine! Joe Bosworth here."

"Hi, Joe, I need to ask you something."

"Sunshine, I only have a few minutes before Evelyn and I jump on a plane. I'm glad you called. There's something I want to talk to you about," Joe said cheerfully.

"Sure, what's up?" Jannika asked.

"Jannika, I won't beat around the bush. I'm going to sell the store."

"Sell the store?" Jannika's stomach dropped. What Gunnie had heard was true. The floor seemed to disappear under her feet.

"Yes. I'm buying a fishing boat in Florida. Going to do charter fishing trips. Hire a captain, the whole bit. Isn't it exciting?"

Jannika felt the color drain from her face.

"Oh…well…when is this going to happen?" Jannika felt her throat tighten. Not her store. She couldn't lose her store. One by one the future losses bubbled up in her mind. Everything she'd tried so hard not to think about ever since she heard the gossip. Her book groups, Sarah, her customers, the Purple Tent ladies, the books, the other shop owners, her new life. Her stomach turned and she felt queasy.

"I'm going to put things in motion as soon as we get back from Florida, next month. We won't close right away—we'll need to take inventory, then put it on the market and see if we get any bites. I say it will take a month to get organized, then she'll go up for sale. Bon voyage. Get it? Hey, what did you want to ask me?"

"I wanted to ask about the store. But now I know." She sat down. Her hands were trembling.

"Hey, sunshine, sorry to cut this short, but I have to run. We'll talk more when I get back. Bye, now!"

"Wait, but—" Jannika said to dead air. Joe had already ended the call. She needed to talk to someone about this. Jannika got her cell phone out of her pocket and called Aunt Gunnie.

This is Gunilla Johnson. If you're hearing this message I am either asleep or out somewhere havin' fun. Call me back. I don't like returning messages unless it's an emergency.

"Damn it," she whispered.

An hour later, the store was finally quiet, with one lone reader left in the back. Probably just a lull, but she appreciated the break. Her phone chimed a text. She scanned the screen—Marcy.

The parents love you I'm sure. Was there romance on the mountaintop? Can't wait to tell you about my Thanksgiving... with Amy... and both of my PARENTS.

She replied, *Big story. Too big. Can you call me?*

Sure.

Two seconds later, her phone played a cha-cha, Marcy's ringtone.

"It's been crazy busy here today. If any customers come, I'll have to let you go."

"Righty-o. I know the drill," Marcy said.

She quietly filled Marcy in on her Thanksgiving with Lee, and Joe Bosworth's phone call.

"Jeez, Nick, I don't know what to say. You were having the best Thanksgiving of your life, and you left? Your boss is selling the store? Since when? How are you? That's probably a stupid question."

Jannika waved at the last customer as he was leaving the store.

"I got really overwhelmed by the big family, and Lee, and everything, and I told Lee I needed a break. I need to figure some stuff out. Aunt Gunnie and I had a good talk after we left, and I finally called Joe Bosworth to see if the rumors were true, and they are. He's selling the store." Future scenarios were flipping like flashcards through her mind. Jannika working at the local drugstore. Jannika homeless. Jannika moving back with her mother. Jannika getting in her car and driving and driving…

"I love how you always say *Joe Bosworth* like he's a company or something. Should I push you about Lee or let it be right now?"

"Are you driving? You sound like you're in the car. I need to get away and be by myself and come up with a plan, figure out how I feel."

"Not driving, but I'm in the car. Do you want to be away, away? I can check with my mom and see if the cabin is free this weekend. I think everyone has plans at other places."

"I feel like everything is falling apart, like, in pieces. Like I'm in pieces. Like I touch things and they shatter."

"Hey, hey, I think you are getting way ahead of yourself there, kiddo. You know what I think?"

"What?"

"If you're still at the store, close early, pick up some food, feed yourself, and go to bed. But at least text Lee and let her know you're okay. You don't have to do anything for the rest of the day. No decisions, no confrontations. Just take care of Nick. Okay? I'll get in touch with my mom tonight and find out about the cabin."

"You're a smarty-pants."

"You'll be okay."

"Will I?" Jannika did not feel like things would be okay. She felt like the ground beneath her feet had shifted and she was staring into an open hole.

"No matter what happens, I know you'll be okay."

"Thanks, Marce, that helps. My store—what am I going to do?"

"Nothing tonight. Promise me. Please go home and take care of you and get some shut-eye."

"I will. How did your holiday go, with Amy and your parents?"

"They were gracious and actually seemed warm, which is amazing. Especially my..." Jannika read the hesitation in Marcy's silence. "My dad. After Amy left, my dad had a little talk with me about how he's concerned about how the lesbo daughter and her girlfriend might look, and he hoped it didn't affect business. I took a deep breath and was going to plow into him, but my mom saved the day. She was incredible." Marcy hesitated again. "She reminded him that we have quite a few gay and lesbian employees and what it will mean to them and their families to know that their workplace is welcoming. Then she winked at me and said she had been doing her homework and was learning the lingo. She actually said *lingo*."

Jannika laughed as tears slid over her cheeks and dripped onto her shirt. Maybe sometimes broken things could be fixed. Maybe always planning for the worst possible outcome was no longer protecting her heart, but preventing her from finding happiness. Maybe.

CHAPTER TWENTY-FOUR

The next morning, Jannika tried to concentrate on her work, but her eyes welled up when she looked at anything in the store. Sarah did most of the customer service work. Jannika worked at the computer, entering books into their inventory system. That was the first thing Joe Bosworth said he'd do before he sold the store—take inventory of everything. She clenched her teeth.

"Sarah, could you come here a minute?"

"Be right there, boss."

She heard some shuffling at the back of the store and Sarah sprinted up the women's fiction/mystery aisle.

"Sarah, I know there's a lot going on here. If I can get you some help, would you be okay picking up a few extra hours and running the store for me for a few days? I really need to get away and do some heavy-duty thinking."

Sarah peered at her so sharply that Jannika started to feel a little weird. "You know, I can't feel your usual energy wavelets ever since you came back after Thanksgiving with Lee. I know something's wrong. If I can help you by running the store for you, then that's how the universe is wanting me to help. The universe spreads out the choices in front of me and lets me decide." Sarah brought her hands out in front of her and opened her arms wide.

"Thanks, and I can't talk about it right now. I'm going to call Vicki and Linda. I think Vicki is home most days now. Would you be okay with that?"

"She's a little intense, but it's okay. I'll bring her some valerian tea and that might help. Where are you going?"

"I'm hoping to go up to Marcy's cabin for a few days," Jannika said.

"Nature is our mother-healer."

"Thanks, Sarah." She phoned Vicki, and she was available and happy to help. She heard Linda in the background and thought she sounded pretty happy about Vicki being out of the house too.

Jannika continued working on returning phone calls from people who wanted to trade books for store credit, a practice she was phasing out because it was an administrative nightmare. Now if someone brought in really great books, she might give them a gift certificate to the store, but only if the books were exceptional and she knew they would sell within a few months.

She grabbed her Fairlee Diner coffee mug from the shelf behind her and plugged in the electric tea kettle. She decided on Earl Grey and plopped the tea bag in her mug. As the water heated, she looked out the window that faced Main Street. Her body felt numb. No racing heart. No sweaty palms. Her thoughts and feelings seemed buried in mud. She needed time alone to uncover them and sort through things.

She texted Lee: *Sorry I haven't called. Just heard boss is selling the store for sure. I'm going to get away for a few days. Lots to think about. I'll let you know when I'm coming back, but I need some time alone to sort things out.*

A few minutes later, Lee replied, *Thanks for letting me know. I'm so sorry about the store. Please let me know if you need anything. Anything at all.*

Jannika's phone did the cha-cha.

"Hey, tall Swedish babe. I found out about the cabin."

"Thanks for trying to make me smile," she replied. Marcy really was the best.

"You can use the cabin. Mom said it's available the next ten days." Silence on the line, then, "Maybe I could get away for a few days and go up there with you."

"Thanks, Marce, but I need to have some space to figure out how I'm feeling and what I'm going to do. And I love you, but I need to do this alone."

"Are you okay to be alone up at the cabin? I know you know the area, we went there enough times hiking and getting our lesbian legs in shape to chase women."

"Yup."

"It's that bad? I thought I'd at least get a chuckle or a sarcastic reply."

"Sorry, my head is someplace else. Do I need to bring anything besides bedding and food? I've got store coverage for five days, if that's okay."

"You need more help? I'm at the ready. Dad can spare me for a few days. I don't know the books real well, but I can chat up almost anyone."

"Yes, you can. Thanks, but Vicki's covering. She's filled in once before."

"Vicki? My friend Vicki the trash mouth is going to run your store? You chose her over me? No, we can at least share the wealth. Vicki for two days, then I'll take three. We'll let Sarah boss us around. Well, I will, anyway."

"I know you're busy at work and with Amy." Part of Jannika felt like she was abandoning her store and imposing on her friends, but she knew she needed time and space to get clear about things and was grateful for the cabin and her friends.

"It's done. I'll let Vicki know. And do I have permission to fire her if she alienates all the customers?"

"Marcy Barclay, I love you." This must be what it felt like to have a sister.

"Love you too, kiddo. I still know the drill from the weekend I helped Sarah out, plus she'll be there, right? We'll keep the ship afloat for you. But promise me something, Nick, okay?"

"Sure, what?"

"If you start feeling creepy up there or lonesome or sick or anything, text me. We have a good signal up there, and you know me, phone is on my hip twenty-four-seven. Or close to my hip, anyways."

"Promise."

"And no hiking alone up in the sticks this time of year. Stay on the path in that little ridge by the pines on the hill out back. There's good cell service on the ridge, but you're still in the woods. And wear some color—it's still hunting season."

"Got it. Promise number two."

"Take care of yourself, Nick. You'll get to the other side of this."

"I hope so."

❖

She spent her first day at the cabin putting away groceries and fixing up the little bedroom off the kitchen with her reading light, favorite sheets, and the paisley patchwork quilt Aunt Gunnie made her when she was thirteen. She brought it out when she needed to feel close to her aunt. She needed some of her strength now. The first night she cried and took a bath and cried some more.

In the morning of the second day, she brought in wood for the woodstove. She kept bringing in wood until her arms felt like two pieces of oak. She stacked the wood near the stove and along the living room wall and over by the front door. She stacked it in the kitchen and in the back hallway outside the bedroom she was using. The repetitive physicality of hauling wood from the woodshed to the house, and the stillness of the little cabin in the snow, quieted Jannika's mind and her heart.

At night she sat by the woodstove with a crocheted afghan she found in the bedroom closet and a spiral-bound notebook. She drew columns. She made lists. She thought if she could map out a plan for her future after the store, she could sort out her feelings for Lee. But every idea brought her back to Lee. She tried to sort through her emotions, examining each one like she would pages in an old book in Edgar's store.

She'd asked Edgar once why he put so much time and money into repairing books that no one might buy. He told her he did it because he loved the books. *Love is always unquestionably worth it, my dear.*

After lunch on the third day, she found a pair of snowshoes and some ski poles in the back hallway, along with a blaze orange hat and gloves, and decided to give snowshoes a try again after all these years. All the summer and fall hikes with Marcy paid off as she lifted her snowshoe-clad feet and felt the stretch along her glutes. She made her way through the small field in back of the cabin and found the trail that wound its way through the pine trees and up a hill.

She stood on the rise surrounded by white pines. From this height, the cabin looked like one of those country snow scene jigsaw puzzles Aunt Gunnie always had on her card table in her back sewing room. A small plume of white smoke rose from the chimney, and around the cabin were what looked like mounds of snow, but she knew they were the two woodsheds and the old outhouse. Jannika's hands were cold and stiff. She started down the trail. She couldn't escape it. If she hiked up the hill, she had to come down. If she stayed at the cabin, eventually she'd have to go back to Grangeton and face the store being sold. And Lee. Aunt Gunnie and Marcy had faith in her ability to make these decisions. She took a few more snowy steps on the ridge path.

Her hand covered her heart. She thought about how free and balanced she'd felt in the woods at Watts Lake, walking side by side with Lee. She planted her poles at her sides and put her hands on her hips. Marcy called that the Wonder Woman pose. And she decided right then that she didn't want to run away or hide away from life. She wanted to face life head-on. She knew in her heart that no matter what happened with the store, or how difficult that loss might be, Lee would stand by her side. And that was exactly where she wanted Lee to be. By her side.

A twig cracked behind Jannika and she spun around. "Not too jumpy, am I?" she said to the forest. Her eye caught the flash of the white backside of a deer disappearing into the trees. The trail wove in and out of the pine forest and down the side of the hill. She turned, and the back of one snowshoe caught on the other. She went down on her side and untangled her feet.

"Damn it. Really?" Her hands fumbled for her poles. "Really, Nick?" She stood up, put her poles to one side, and tried to brush snow off with snowy gloves. She laughed out loud, then snowshoed down the trail to the cabin. She was going home tomorrow morning.

Chapter Twenty-five

Jannika woke an hour before the alarm went off. She'd cleaned the cabin and packed the night before. She ate a cup of instant oatmeal and poured the rest of her tea into her travel mug. Then she texted Lee and Sarah and Marcy to tell them she was coming home today.

Lee sent one line back: *Can we talk later?*

Jannika replied without hesitation, *Yes.*

She drove directly to The Pageturner from the cabin and got to work a half hour early. She walked around the store and thought everything looked just fine. There was one odd display of fish books, but she figured Sarah must have let Marcy or Vicki be creative. She turned on the lights, made the coffee, and saw the large pile of mail on her desk. Actually, two piles of mail.

During the two-hour drive she'd rehearsed what she wanted to say to Lee when she called her. She didn't feel quite as brave here as she did at the cabin. Sitting in the store and looking at all she was going to say good-bye to made her stomach flutter. She moved a small stack of paperbacks and the mail pile started to slide off the desk. She saw a familiar return address on an envelope that was now on the floor. It was a letter from Edgar. Edgar never wrote her. Something must be wrong. She tore open the envelope.

My dearest Jannika,

I heard through the bookseller grapevine that Bosworth was looking to sell The Pageturner. I have a business proposition for you to consider. I have a buyer for the book—yes, that book. Someone has been interested in it for quite some time and told me if I ever found a reason to part with it, to please let him have first offer. I've always thought we made a great bookselling team, and I'm prepared to buy The Pageturner together with you (I know you have a small nest egg as well)—equal partners. You would continue to manage the store, and I'm quite sure it will continue to be successful—in bookseller measure.

I purposefully didn't call or visit you with this proposal because I want you to consider this carefully, and I want you to know that I've already sold the book and have pocketed the money. (I also knew the look and the talking-to I would get when I told you that.) I'm looking for an investment for this money, and I know of no more stable investment than you, my dear. Helen and I would be very disappointed if we weren't able to complete this transaction. I would be a bookstore mogul of a kind. With two bookstores, one in the great state of Maine and one with you in New Hampshire, how could we not succeed?

Felicitations,

Edgar

Jannika's hands shook as she read the letter a second time. Tears filled her eyes. Oh, Edgar, no. Not *the* book. "He's done it. He won't undo it, I know him. Oh, that wonderful man."

Someone knocked at the door.

Jannika wiped her eyes and saw Andy from the bakery. She signaled just-a-minute, folded the letter, and went to the door to unlock it.

He passed her a box. "Special delivery. I was supposed to get it to you right before you opened today. I'm supposed to leave it with you, no one else."

"Thanks, Andy. Well, as you can see, it's me. Let me get my bag and get you something."

"Oh, that's okay, Jannika. We're just down the street. I've got to get back, though." Andy turned and left.

"All right," Jannika called after him. "Thanks."

She remembered another bakery delivery a few weeks ago and her heart picked up speed to think whatever was in the box might be from Lee. She cut the string with her scissors and opened the box. A half dozen oatmeal raisin cookies and an envelope. Today must be her day for letters. Well, it couldn't be bad news if she sent her cookies, right? She opened the envelope, took out the letter, and unfolded it. Her face crumpled. She shook her head from side to side in disbelief. It wasn't a letter from Lee.

And Leslie, I know I'm younger than you, and it might seem like we're very different, but I don't think so, not underneath. From the first moment I saw you, I knew in my heart that you are my soul mate and that we're supposed to be together forever. I love you with my heart, my breath, my bones, and with all my soul. You are the most beautiful person I have ever seen. The world looks more beautiful when I'm with you and I feel like I can do anything. If you have any feelings for me at all please let me know. Here is my—

Jannika couldn't see to read anymore. Tears streamed down her face. She couldn't believe that Lee kept this letter all those years. And Jannika knew she felt the same now as she had eighteen years ago. She loved this woman with all her heart. Every bit of her believed that they were meant to be together. She knew she couldn't predict the future. But she wanted to be with Lee, whatever that future would be. She needed to call Lee. Now. Before she had to open the store.

She took her phone from her back pocket and called her.

"Hey there," Lee said.

"I got the cookies." Jannika's nose was running. She sniffed. "I can't believe you still had that letter. After all this time."

"I used to take that letter out every once in a while and read it. I thought you might not remember it."

"Of course I do. I remember everything, Lee."

"I do too and I'm also happy that I'm learning new things about you, like your weakness for oatmeal raisin cookies. I'm glad you're back. It's really good to hear your voice," Lee said.

"It's good to hear yours too. But I don't want to talk about things on the phone. I want to see you. How do you feel about coming over tonight for dinner? If you're free, I mean. I just got some really good news. Fantastic news. I want to celebrate with you. Edgar is going to help me buy the store. Can you believe it?"

"Oh my gosh, really? That's incredible, so wonderful for you. When did you find out? Yes, I want to talk too and celebrate with you. Tonight?"

"It feels not quite real. I just opened a letter he sent to the store, right before I got the cookies." Jannika touched the letter on her desk. "I've got to open. Is six okay? I can't leave early—Sarah and everyone have worked a lot of hours for me." All of a sudden six o'clock seemed very far away. She wanted to see Lee now. She didn't want to wait another second.

"You go open your store. *Your store*, Nick! You must be so excited. I can't wait to hear about everything. I'll see you tonight."

"Okay, I'll see you later." Jannika put her phone on her desk and walked around, opening the store. She looked at everything that made her feel such terrible impending loss just a little while ago, and now it all glowed with possibilities. She didn't need to take time to think about it. She would love to be Edgar's partner. The relief of not having to leave her store washed through her and was replaced by happiness. She needed to call Aunt Gunnie. And Marcy. But first she needed to call Edgar and Helen.

She picked up her phone and a cookie, took a bite, and smiled. She leaned back in her desk chair and put her feet up on the desk, crossing them at the ankles. "My store." Then she quickly took her feet off the desk before any customers came in.

Lee's hands shook a little as she placed her phone back in the case attached to the waistband of her jeans. She was happy about Jannika's store, but she wasn't sure she wanted to see her tonight. She'd tried to be patient like her sister suggested, but the past week had been awful. She didn't like not knowing what was going on with Jannika. She wasn't a worrier, but she wasn't sure the right thing to do when she heard Jannika was coming back a couple of days early. Was that good news? Bad news? She wanted to send a message with the cookies and the letter, that their relationship didn't just start a few weeks ago.

She poured herself a cup of coffee and sat down at the farmhouse table. She looked out the window at the fields. Maybe she should call Jannika back and wait a few days, until the excitement from the bookstore news had settled in. Maybe she would still need space after that. Maybe Jannika would keep needing space, the kind of space that never let a person get anywhere close to an intimate relationship.

Lee got up and walked into the living room. She looked at her carved animals lined up on the mantel and the ones that sat on the shelves. She'd lived alone for a long time now. She had a pretty predictable pattern of work, chores, visiting her family up north, and hanging out with friends once in a while. Taking a chance hadn't been a question she'd been face-to-face with in a number of years. She picked up a small baby owl carving.

"Hey, baby wise one, what do you think? Should I go to dinner tonight and see what happens?" She put the owl to her ear. "Yup, I knew you were going to say that."

Chapter Twenty-six

Jannika set the timer on the oven for forty-five minutes. That's what Jeannie at Heavenly Homemade Meals told her. After she invited Lee to dinner, she remembered she didn't have any food in the house. She could live on Heavenly's meals if she could afford to. Every single thing she'd tried was delicious, like it was made by your favorite grandmother. She'd picked up the lasagna, a green salad, and a loaf of crusty Italian bread. She had just a few minutes to change clothes before Lee came over.

She'd spent most of the day thinking about owning The Pageturner and the changes she would make. Auntie and Marcy and Sarah were so happy for her. She kept replaying Edgar and Helen's conversation in her mind. Helen was on the other line mostly just listening in. They were overjoyed that Jannika accepted their offer and told her that she was family. They were so happy that all three of them would be sharing this project.

Jannika saw headlights coming down her driveway. Her heart pounded. It was one thing to decide how you felt about a person. It was quite another to have to face that person and tell them. She was excited to see Lee. It felt like they had been apart for weeks, but it was only days. She opened the door just as Lee stepped on the front step.

Would the sight of Lee always take her breath away? She couldn't think of anything to say. She forgot why she was standing there. Lee broke the silence with her smile.

"Hey, beautiful," Lee said. "Can I come in?"

"Yes, sorry. I'm so…"

Lee touched the back of her elbow on her way in the cottage and Jannika felt goose bumps run up her arm and the back of her head. Butterflies flew circles in her stomach and her breath quickened. She closed the door behind Lee. Too many words tried to come out of her mouth at once.

"Do you want to go…to do…" She shook her head and took a deep breath. "Sorry. Let me start again. Hi, Lee. I'm so glad to see you. I've got lasagna in the oven and salad on the table all ready for us. Are you hungry?"

Lee stepped toward Jannika and looked into her eyes. "Everything is okay, Nick. And yes, I'm very hungry."

Jannika didn't know if Lee meant that to sound so sexy, but her body took notice.

"Okay. Let's have salad, and I'll tell you about the store first. Then I want to talk about us."

Jannika told Lee about her fears about losing the store and how after spending time at the cabin and talking with her aunt she realized that if she lost the store it would be devastating, but she would survive it, because she had a pretty good track record at not only surviving, but taking care of herself well. Then she told her about getting to the store this morning and finding the letter.

"I'm still just a little upset that Edgar sold that book. But once I heard Edgar's voice and Helen's voice, I was over that. I was just happy. This is my dream, since I was a little girl—to own my own bookstore. And it's going to happen. Thanks to Edgar. We work so well together. I can't wait for you to meet him."

"You want me to meet him?" Lee asked just as the timer went off for the lasagna.

"Yes." Jannika got up and pulled their supper out of the oven. "Big piece or small piece?" Jannika was hoping that concentrating on this task would help her figure out how to tell Lee what she wanted to tell her.

"Small piece. Even though I'm pretty hungry, I don't really feel like eating."

Jannika cut the pieces and brought them to the table.

"I missed you," Jannika said.

"I missed you too." Lee picked up her fork and poked at the lasagna. "I know you needed to be alone, and I respect that, but it was hard to be here wanting to help you or listen."

"I'm sorry I left your family's Thanksgiving like that." Jannika felt like her heart would pound out of her chest. She thought of herself on the ridge at the cabin in her Wonder Woman pose. She knew she could do this. "Your family is everything I always dreamed a family would be like. All of a sudden it was like everything I had ever wanted was right in front of me. It overwhelmed me and I got scared. Aunt Gunnie and I talked, and that helped me sort things a bit. Then I heard about the store and knew I needed time away from everyone to get clear about my feelings."

"Thanks for telling me that. I know you're sorted out about the store. What about us?"

She knew it was the right time to take that chance. She put down her fork and said, "I can't eat anymore, what about you? I don't want to be across a table from you right now."

"I can't eat anything else, either." Lee got up from the table and took their plates into the kitchen.

Jannika went to Lee, took her by the hand, and led her to the couch. They sat down and turned to each other. She stroked the back of Lee's hand with her thumb.

Lee said, "It was important to me to share that letter with you. I wanted you to know I kept it." Lee smoothed the palm of her other hand on her thigh.

Jannika looked into Lee's eyes. "About the letter." Jannika felt like her heart would pound right out of her chest. Her hands felt sweaty and she felt a little out of breath.

"Yes?"

"When I read that letter again, my first reaction was embarrassment that as a kid I just laid it all out there, my heart wide open. And what did I know? I was just seventeen. I had only had one girlfriend at that point. But my second reaction was, yes. Yes, that's exactly how I feel about Lee. I love her. I love you. You are my soul mate, and I do think we're supposed to be together forever. I want to build a life with you by my side." Jannika's eyes filled with tears and she edged closer to Lee. She felt exhilarated when she saw Lee's cautious look slide into a smile that made all the fractured pieces of her world come together into one whole.

"Oh, Nick." Lee leaned toward Jannika and took her other hand. "I want to make sure you have all the facts where I'm concerned."

"All the facts?"

"The facts of my heart. Fact one: I love you. I'm in love with you. Fact two: I want you in my life always, as in forever always. Starting right now. Fact three: I know, in the exact same way that I know my name, that we belong together. When I walked into the bookstore and saw that wonderful, beautiful, passionate girl grown into this incredible woman, I knew my heart would never be the same again. I love you with every bit of myself. I love you, Nick. I want to go outside and tell the stars and the trees and the fields that I love you."

"Let's do it," Jannika said pulling Lee from the couch. "Let's go tell the world."

She opened the door and led Lee outside. She looked up at the sky and said, "I love Lee Thompson!"

Lee looked at the trees surrounding Jannika's cottage. "Hey, trees, I love Jannika Peterson!" She laughed, let go of Jannika's hand, and put her arm around her waist.

Jannika turned toward Lee and stepped closer. She put her arms around Lee's neck and bent her head to kiss her. "I love you, Lee," she whispered, her lips barely touching Lee's.

"I love you, Nick." Lee's lips moved over Jannika's.

They kissed slowly, exploring each other's lips.

The tip of Jannika's tongue teased the inside of Lee's lips and Lee held Jannika tighter, bringing her stomach and thighs into contact with Lee's.

"Inside." The word came out in one breath. Jannika walked backward to the door of the cottage, her lips never leaving Lee's. She fumbled with the doorknob as Lee moved her hand from her back to her hip, then she squeezed her hip and Jannika let go of the doorknob as her knees buckled. "Okay, okay, let's get inside." She turned and opened the door.

Once they were inside, Jannika closed the door and turned to kiss Lee again.

Lee tipped her head and kissed Jannika's collarbone as she ran her hands up under Jannika's shirt. Jannika's back arched in response. She tried to grab Lee's sweater and lift it over her head, but Lee had lifted Jannika's shirt up above her bra and was kissing her chest with long slow kisses while she held Jannika's hips, rubbing her thumbs on Jannika's hipbones.

Jannika had no thoughts except how to show Lee what she was feeling through her lips and hands and body.

"Let me get your sweater off," Jannika said.

Lee let go of Jannika's hips and helped her pull her sweater over her head. When Lee's hands were over her head, Jannika started kissing her and touching her breasts through her bra. Lee's nipples stood out beneath the fabric and Jannika bent her head to kiss first one, then the other.

"Come to my lair." Jannika smiled and led Lee to her bedroom. She knelt on the floor and unbuttoned and unzipped Lee's jeans. "Help me, just a little," she said as she pulled Lee's pants down to her ankles, kissing the waistband of Lee's underwear as her hands slid back up Lee's legs and moved to the inside of her thighs. Jannika could feel Lee's thighs tremble under her touch.

Lee touched Jannika's hair. "I need to kiss you and I need to get on that bed before my legs give out."

Jannika stood up and took off all her clothes while she watched Lee's face.

Lee lay on her side on the bed. "I'll never get tired of looking at you. Come here." Lee moved over and Jannika got on the bed and lay facing Lee.

She reached for Lee and kissed her shoulder while she undid Lee's bra and helped her slip it off. Her lips moved across Lee's shoulder and down to her breast. Jannika heard Lee's breath quicken as she continued to trace her tongue over Lee's breast, circling the nipple and kissing it softly. Her hand caressed Lee's lower back and her fingers moved lower.

"Not so fast, Nick." Lee's voice was husky and low. She shifted her weight, so Jannika moved away from her and onto her back. Lee moved on top of her and kissed her.

Jannika felt the kiss travel down her middle and settle between her legs. Her hips arched and Lee groaned.

"I want you. I want us. Together." Jannika's words, face, and body asked Lee the question.

Lee lay back on her side facing Jannika and stroked her side, drew circles on her hip, and slid her hand down the outside of her thigh while Jannika teased Lee's left breast and moved her hand down Lee's stomach to her hip and the outside of her thigh. Lee parted her legs but didn't take her eyes away from Jannika's.

Jannika felt Lee's hand move in the same way as Jannika's, mirroring the motion. Lee's hand was on the outside of her thigh. Jannika parted her legs and as she slid her hand to the inside of Lee's thigh, she felt Lee's hand move to the inside of hers. She let out a soft cry but kept her eyes on Lee. She knew Lee could feel the love pouring from her eyes. She moved her hand higher. Her face was inches from Lee's. Her fingers moved higher and touched Lee's wetness, and she felt Lee's fingers ready to move inside of her. Her hips arched to get closer to Lee.

Lee's fingers reached a little higher and found what they were looking for.

"Nick, oh, honey." She groaned as Jannika's fingers slid up inside her.

Jannika couldn't hold eye contact any longer. She threw her head back and her hips responded to Lee's touch. Her excitement grew as she touched Lee and Lee's body convulsed with desire and release. In that moment her awareness tunneled to the passion she felt as her body arched and her hips drove down into Lee's touch.

Lee gently moved Jannika onto her back and stroked her lightly with her fingertips. Jannika put an arm out and Lee put her head on Jannika's chest as Jannika wrapped her arm around her.

"Wow," Jannika whispered.

"Wow, indeed," Lee said. "You are incredible." She moved her hand to stroke Jannika's thigh.

"That was intense. Can I tell you something?"

"Anything, my love." Lee shifted so she could look at Jannika's face.

"That felt like…This might sound silly, but it felt like we joined forces or something."

Lee's smile covered her face.

"Did you feel it?" When Lee looked at her as they were making love, it was like the love that passed between them sealed their connection.

"To me it felt like we've been carrying this bond around for all these years, kind of like those necklaces with the two pieces that only fit each other. It felt like our pieces found each other and bonded." Lee traced Jannika's forehead with her fingers as she looked at her.

"You felt it too, then." Jannika smiled and gently pulled Lee down to kiss her.

"I did indeed," Lee said and sealed it with a kiss.

About the Author

Laney Webber has lived in four of the six New England states. Her love affair with reading and books began when she read the line, "Sit, Spot, Sit!" in her first grade class. Laney lives in Vermont with her wife; their rescue dog, Gracie; and their rescue cat, Rudy Valentino. She works as a librarian, which gives her free access to shelves and shelves of books. She believes that libraries are the best places to visit on the planet. When Laney doesn't have a book or pen in her hand, she likes to camp and wander around New England.

Books Available from Bold Strokes Books

A Chapter on Love by Laney Webber. When Jannika and Lee reunite, their instant connection feels like a gift, but neither is ready for a second chance at love. Will they finally get on the same page when it comes to love? (978-1-63555-366-6)

Drawing Down the Mist by Sheri Lewis Wohl. Everyone thinks Grand Duchess Maria Romanova died in 1918. They were almost right. (978-1-63555-341-3)

Listen by Kris Bryant. Lily Croft is inexplicably drawn to Hope D'Marco but will she have the courage to confront the consequences of her past and present colliding? (978-1-63555-318-5)

Perfect Partners by Maggie Cummings. Elite police dog trainer Sara Wright has no intention of falling in love with a coworker, until Isabel Marquez arrives at Homeland Security's Northeast Regional Training facility and Sara's good intentions start to falter. (978-1-63555-363-5)

Shut Up and Kiss Me by Julie Cannon. What better way to spend two weeks of hell in paradise than in the company of a hot, sexy woman? (978-1-63555-343-7)

Spencer's Cove by Missouri Vaun. When Foster Owen and Abigail Spencer meet they uncover a story of lives adrift, loves lost, and true love found. (978-1-63555-171-6)

Without Pretense by TJ Thomas. After living for decades hiding from the truth, can Ava learn to trust Bianca with her secrets and her heart? (978-1-63555-173-0)

Unexpected Lightning by Cass Sellars. Lightning strikes once more when Sydney and Parker fight a dangerous stranger who threatens the peace they both desperately want. (978-1-163555-276-8)

Emily's Art and Soul by Joy Argento. When Emily meets Andi Marino she thinks she's found a new best friend but Emily doesn't know that Andi is fast falling in love with her. Caught up in exploring her sexuality, will Emily see the only woman she needs is right in front of her? (978-1-63555-355-0)

Escape to Pleasure: Lesbian Travel Erotica edited by Sandy Lowe and Victoria Villasenor. Join these award-winning authors as they explore the sensual side of erotic lesbian travel. (978-1-63555-339-0)

Music City Dreamers by Robyn Nyx. Music can bring lovers together. In Music City, it can tear them apart. (978-1-63555-207-2)

Ordinary is Perfect by D. Jackson Leigh. Atlanta marketing superstar Autumn Swan's life derails when she inherits a country home, a child, and a very interesting neighbor. (978-1-63555-280-5)

Royal Court by Jenny Frame. When royal dresser Holly Weaver's passionate personality begins to melt Royal Marine Captain Quincy's icy heart, will Holly be ready for what she exposes beneath? (978-1-63555-290-4)

Strings Attached by Holly Stratimore. Success. Riches. Music. Passion. It's a life most can only dream of, but stardom comes at a cost. (978-1-63555-347-5)

The Ashford Place by Jean Copeland. When Isabelle Ashford inherits an old house in small-town Connecticut, family secrets, a shocking discovery, and an unexpected romance complicate her plan for a fast profit and a temporary stay. (978-1-63555-316-1)

Treason by Gun Brooke. Zoem Malderyn's existence is a deadly threat to everyone on Gemocon and Commander Neenja KahSandra must find a way to save the woman she loves from having to commit the ultimate sacrifice. (978-1-63555-244-7)

A Wish Upon a Star by Jeannie Levig. Erica Cooper has learned to depend on only herself, but when her new neighbor, Leslie Raymond, befriends Erica's special needs daughter, the walls protecting her heart threaten to crumble. (978-1-63555-274-4)

Answering the Call by Ali Vali. Detective Sept Savoie returns to the streets of New Orleans, as do the dead bodies from ritualistic killings, and she does everything in her power to bring them to justice while trying to keep her partner, Keegan Blanchard, safe. (978-1-63555-050-4)

Breaking Down Her Walls by Erin Zak. Could a love worth staying for be the key to breaking down Julia Finch's walls? (978-1-63555-369-7)

Exit Plans for Teenage Freaks by 'Nathan Burgoine. Cole always has a plan—especially for escaping his small-town reputation as "that kid who was kidnapped when he was four"— but when he teleports to a museum, it's time to face facts: it's possible he's a total freak after all. (978-1-63555-098-6)

Friends Without Benefits by Dena Blake. When Dex Putman gets the woman she thought she always wanted, she soon wonders if it's really love after all. (978-1-63555-349-9)

Invalid Evidence by Stevie Mikayne. Private Investigator Jil Kidd is called away to investigate a possible killer whale, just when her partner Jess needs her most. (978-1-63555-307-9)

Pursuit of Happiness by Carsen Taite. When attorney Stevie Palmer's client reveals a scandal that could derail Senator Meredith Mitchell's presidential bid, their chance at love may be collateral damage. (978-1-63555-044-3)

Seascape by Karis Walsh. Marine biologist Tess Hansen returns to Washington's isolated northern coast where she struggles to adjust to small-town living while courting an endowment for her orca research center from Brittany James. (978-1-63555-079-5)

Second in Command by VK Powell. Jazz Perry's life is disrupted and her career jeopardized when she becomes personally involved with the case of an abandoned child and the child's competent but strict social worker, Emory Blake. (978-1-63555-185-3)

Taking Chances by Erin McKenzie. When Valerie Cruz and Paige Wellington clash over what's in the best interest of the children in Valerie's care, the children may be the ones who teach them it's worth taking chances for love. (978-1-63555-209-6)

All of Me by Emily Smith. When chief surgical resident Galen Burgess meets her new intern, Rowan Duncan, she may finally discover that doing what you've always done will only give you what you've always had. (978-1-63555-321-5)

As the Crow Flies by Karen F. Williams. Romance seems to be blooming all around, but problems arise when a restless ghost emerges from the ether to roam the dark corners of this haunting tale. (978-1-63555-285-0)

Both Ways by Ileandra Young. SPEAR agent Danika Karson races to protect the city from a supernatural threat and must rely on the woman she's trained to despise: Rayne, an achingly beautiful vampire. (978-1-63555-298-0)

Calendar Girl by Georgia Beers. Forced to work together, Addison Fairchild and Kate Cooper discover that opposites really do attract. (978-1-63555-333-8)

Lovebirds by Lisa Moreau. Two women from different worlds collide in a small California mountain town, each with a mission that doesn't include falling in love. (978-1-63555-213-3)

Media Darling by Fiona Riley. Can Hollywood bad girl Emerson and reluctant celebrity gossip reporter Hayley work together to make each other's dreams come true? Or will Emerson's secrets ruin not one career, but two? (978-1-63555-278-2)

Stroke of Fate by Renee Roman. Can Sean Moore live up to her reputation and save Jade Rivers from the stalker determined to end Jade's career and, ultimately, her life? (978-1-63555-62-4)

The Rise of the Resistance by Jackie D. The soul of America has been lost for almost a century. A few people may be the difference between a phoenix rising to save the masses or permanent destruction. (978-1-63555-259-1)

The Sex Therapist Next Door by Meghan O'Brien. At the intersection of sex and intimacy, anything is possible. Even love. (978-1-63555-296-6)

Unforgettable by Elle Spencer. When one night changes a lifetime... Two romance novellas from best-selling author Elle Spencer. (978-1-63555-429-8)

Against All Odds by Kris Bryant, Maggie Cummings, M. Ullrich. Peyton and Tory escaped death once, but will they survive when Bradley's determined to make his kill rate one hundred percent? (978-1-63555-193-8)

Autumn's Light by Aurora Rey. Casual hookups aren't supposed to include romantic dinners and meeting the family. Can Mat Pero see beyond the heartbreak that led her to keep her worlds so separate, and will Graham Connor be waiting if she does? (978-1-63555-272-0)

Breaking the Rules by Larkin Rose. When Virginia and Carmen are thrown together by an embarrassing mistake they find out their stubborn determination isn't so heroic after all. (978-1-63555-261-4)

Broad Awakening by Mickey Brent. In the sequel to *Underwater Vibes*, Hélène and Sylvie find ruts in their road to eternal bliss. (978-1-63555-270-6)

Broken Vows by MJ Williamz. Sister Mary Margaret must reconcile her divided heart or risk losing a love that just might be heaven sent. (978-1-63555-022-1)

Flesh and Gold by Ann Aptaker. Havana, 1952, where art thief and smuggler Cantor Gold dodges gangland bullets and mobsters' schemes while she searches Havana's steamy Red Light district for her kidnapped love. (978-1-63555-153-2)

Isle of Broken Years by Jane Fletcher. Spanish noblewoman Catalina de Valasco is in peril, even before the pirates holding her for ransom sail into seas destined to become known as the Bermuda Triangle. (978-1-63555-175-4)

Love Like This by Melissa Brayden. Hadley Cooper and Spencer Adair set out to take the fashion world by storm. If only they knew their hearts were about to be taken. (978-1-63555-018-4)

Secrets On the Clock by Nicole Disney. Jenna and Danielle love their jobs helping endangered children, but that might not be enough to stop them from breaking the rules by falling in love. (978-1-63555-292-8)

Unexpected Partners by Michelle Larkin. Dr. Chloe Maddox tries desperately to deny her attraction for Detective Dana Blake as they flee from a serial killer who's hunting them both. (978-1-63555-203-4)

BOLDSTROKESBOOKS.COM

Looking for your next great read?

Visit BOLDSTROKESBOOKS.COM
to browse our entire catalog of paperbacks, ebooks,
and audiobooks.

Want the first word on what's new?
Visit our website for event info,
author interviews, and blogs.

Subscribe to our free newsletter for sneak peeks,
new releases, plus first notice of promos
and daily bargains.

SIGN UP AT
BOLDSTROKESBOOKS.COM/signup

Bold Strokes Books
Quality and Diversity in LGBTQ Literature

*Bold Strokes Books is an award-winning publisher
committed to quality and diversity in LGBTQ fiction.*

CPSIA information can be obtained
at www.ICGtesting.com
Printed in the USA
BVHW081723140119
537804BV00001B/19/P

9 781635 553666